PENGUIN BOOKS

CITY OF STRANGERS

Ian MacKenzie was raised in Massachusetts. After graduating from Harvard, he worked as a public high school teacher in Brooklyn, where he still lives. He was born in 1982.

IAN MACKENZIE CITY OF STRANGERS

PENGUIN BOOKS

PENGUIN BOOKS

Published by the Penguin Group
Penguin Group (USA) Inc., 375 Hudson Street, New York, New York 10014, U.S.A.
Penguin Group (Canada), 90 Eglinton Avenue East, Suite 700, Toronto, Ontario, Canada M4P
2Y3 (a division of Pearson Penguin Canada Inc.) · Penguin Books Ltd, 80 Strand, London
WC2R oRL, England · Penguin Ireland, 25 St Stephen's Green, Dublin 2, Ireland (a division
of Penguin Books Ltd) · Penguin Group (Australia), 250 Camberwell Road, Camberwell,
Victoria 3124, Australia (a division of Pearson Australia Group Pty Ltd) · Penguin Books
India Pvt Ltd, 11 Community Centre, Panchsheel Park, New Delhi – 110 017, India · Penguin
Group (NZ), 67 Apollo Drive, Rosedale, North Shore 0632, New Zealand (a division of Pearson
New Zealand Ltd) · Penguin Books (South Africa) (Pty) Ltd, 24 Sturdee Avenue, Rosebank,
Johannesburg 2196, South Africa

Penguin Books Ltd, Registered Offices: 80 Strand, London WC2R oRL, England

First published in Great Britain by Harvill Secker,
an imprint of The Random House Group Limited 2009
Published in Penguin Books 2009

10 9 8 7 6 5 4 3 2 1

LIBRARY OF CONGRESS CATALOGING IN PUBLICATION DATA
MacKenzie, Ian.
City of Strangers / Ian MacKenzie.
p.   cm.
ISBN 978-0-14-311578-6
1. Authors—Fiction.   2. Family—Fiction.   3. Family secrets—Fiction.
4. New York (N.Y.)—Fiction.   5. Psychological fiction.   I. Title.
PS3613.A27259C57 2009
813'.6—dc22   2009012971

Printed in the United States of America

For my mother and father

. . . cities are, by definition, full of strangers. To any one person, strangers are far more common in big cities than acquaintances. More common not just in places of public assembly, but more common at a man's own doorstep.

Jane Jacobs, *The Death and Life of Great American Cities*

1

Sunday morning. The exhausted, somnambulant city hasn't yet risen, although there are exceptions. People with heads still brittle from last night's alcohol toss uneasily in foreign beds, lean on elbows and study new companions for signs of life, listen to the plunks and groans of unfamiliar apartments, search for water. In SoHo and the East Village cafes open for business, laying out trays of glossy pastries and turning on the heat; early-waking joggers in Central Park heave their legs against the bleak air, elevating their heart rates, hoping to add a year or two. The unshaven men who run the all-night delis haven't slept. Weekend visitors, impatient to get out before the cholesterol of automobiles clogs every lane, roll up the F.D.R. and the Henry Hudson and then over the bridges, back to Connecticut and Massachusetts. The light is gray. The buses are a quarter full. Delivery trucks prowl the island. And it's the hour of church — mothers and fathers march young children, clothed in suits they will soon outgrow, toward the high doors. From the opposite side of the street, the crowd is a tessellated sea of backs, a dark, undulating mosaic. They blow into fists, press knees together; it is the middle of February and still quite cold. Snow snags in hair but vanishes on the pavement. At the entrance the priest clasps shoulders and lifts children to examine them. Behind a pair of heavy eyeglasses he wears an expression of waxy, pious delight; eruptions of pink skin, squeezed out by the tight collar, bulge under his chin. One of the parishioners says something that amuses him and his outsized laugh explodes from the doors of the church.

Paul Metzger, who has paused to watch, and who grips a cup of coffee with both hands, now walks away, up the avenue and toward his destination, a doorman building tucked into a tree-lined block on the Upper West Side. Like each of Manhattan's territories, one feels, its character starts to form at the edges, in the creases of adjoining neighborhoods, a penumbra of affluence; as one walks north on Amsterdam or Columbus, the glum, stocky housing projects and discount drugstores delicately fall away, revealing the bright, scrubbed memory of a European epitome – chaste, elegant, Italianate. This isn't unfamiliar territory for Paul, who has spent almost his entire life across the river in Brooklyn, yet when he's here he can never quite shake the feeling of being a guest. Its shops cater to habits of dress, diet, and leisure he hasn't got the money for. Even the buildings in which people actually live, with fronts of chalky stone and apple-colored brick, dollhouse doors and wrought-iron roof trim, suggest permanent, historic value. They press out from the smoke-white sky, as heavy as paint. Christmas lights, out of season, thread the bare branches.

He reaches the address he wants and stands for a moment at the entrance, his face fragile and cold, and his body angled against the building in a posture of vaguely hostile indecision. Finally, he goes in and speaks to the doorman, and then, taking the elevator, sails up through the building's core before being made to wait at a second, locking door in the foyer. Its bolts come out with snappish reluctance, and the man who gloomily fills the door frame claps Paul with a hard look of recognition. It has been three years, at least. The math of those years, the additions and subtractions, is immediately apparent, and startling to see in someone more than twenty years older than himself: the crest of thick black hair now sports a prominent white surf; his face is newly lined around the eyes, and in certain places newly indistinct, even soft. He wears glasses. He has the barren, guarded look of a man who hasn't been getting sleep. Paul's mind struggles as it revises the outdated memory. But much has stayed the same. He is tall, sturdy, broad-shouldered, affluently solid at the waist. Paul says something about running late. This isn't the case, as far as he knows, but in his brother's presence he always feels the need to apologize for something.

'I still don't know why I agreed to see you.'

'Jesus, Ben. I'm not even in the door yet.'

Ben, expressionless, watches him, then steps aside. He asks Paul to remove his shoes, a point of etiquette that wouldn't occur to him in his own apartment, and Paul, in socks, feels awkward and vulnerable. His brother points him toward a sofa of immaculate white, a soft island amid the modern, industrial furnishings: the long and heavy-looking mirror that hangs above his head, the glass coffee table, the metal bookshelves. Framed photographs add a grace note of life. Ben goes to the wall and flips something, which starts the whirring of a tiny, delicate motor; as the light shifts around him, Paul realizes that the curtains are parting. He looks out across Central Park, beyond which are the museums and craggy avenues of apartments, and beyond those the outer boroughs – brown, low, wrinkled, gray. The window-panes are teary with snow. In the room's center stands Ben, his arms crossed like a buckle.

'How bad is it for you?' Paul asks.

Ben moves to the window and, with his back to Paul, touches the glass. He runs a hedge fund and has lately come under investigation for insider trading, but Paul, who has never had much of an interest in Ben's work, knows only what he's read in the papers — that reporters are interested at all attests to the seriousness of the affair.

Ben says, 'Are you still in that place by Prospect Park? You've been there what, a year?'

'Ten months.'

'You're all settled in? The rent is reasonable?'

'The rent's fine.'

'You should wait to buy — prices are through the roof. Only an idiot would invest right now.'

'I wasn't contemplating it.'

Ben rubs his jaw. 'Good.' After a pause, he asks, 'A woman?'

He means a girlfriend. Ben has been married to the same woman for two decades; the ambiguity and reversals of unmarried romance are long behind him. His friends no doubt all have wives as well, even if, in a world like Ben's, a few of them must entertain the occasional uncodified sexual encounter.

'No,' says Paul. He hopes this ends the discussion.

Ben nods. 'That's sensible. It's only been a year.'

'Ten months.'

'Right. Somebody in your situation has to move slowly.'

Unlike most brothers, at least as Paul imagines them, he and Ben have no reservoir of shared experience to fall back on, no fixed mold of conversation into which to pour their anxieties when they meet. They were born a generation apart. When Ben was ten his mother divorced their father and he went to live with her; later he took his mother's maiden name, Wald, as his own. She died five years ago. At Ben's instruction, Paul, who met her only once, didn't attend the funeral. He tries asking about Ben's son.

'He's fine,' says Ben. 'Starting his sophomore year at Yale.'

The last time Paul saw Jake was at his bar mitzvah. He

remembers the day well: it's the only bar mitzvah he's ever attended. Ben, a convert, and his wife belong to a Reform temple, and the proceedings were far less tedious than Paul had anticipated. At the door he deliberated briefly before accepting the yarmulke he was offered — better secretly to offend the God he did not believe in than openly to offend the believers in his presence. For the duration of the service he kept reaching up to make sure it hadn't fallen off. His nephew was stiff with nerves at the altar. At the party afterward Paul had too much wine and in the late stages submitted himself to a lecture from Ben, one of the many occasions on which he reminded him that they are only half-brothers; that they share a father but not a mother.

Elsewhere in the apartment a door closes.

'Is Beth home?'

'She's out with her sister.' Ben waits a beat, floating his lie, then walks to the other side of the room. 'You said you wanted to talk about Frank.'

'He isn't doing well. We're talking days, not weeks.'

'So you said.'

'I'm going straight to the hospital from here.' When Ben says nothing, he adds, 'He's your father, too.'

A tectonic movement in Ben's face suggests the turning of inner gears as he suppresses the things he could say. Even as he approaches sixty, Ben remains formidable. His back is straight and he still has a wrestler's chest. When he speaks, his eyebrows, thick as paintbrushes, flex sharply beneath the promontory of his brow — an outward indication of a mind as strong as the body. One look at this man, in his home, surrounded by the things his life's work has earned him, the order and the cleanliness, the framed photographs of a handsome family, the good furniture and expensive electronics, the authority that comes from living well and treating the people he loves decently — one look, and Paul knows it's hopeless. His brother has no reason to leave this. He has no reason to come to a hospital and watch the man he hates most in the world die.

'I've never asked you to be my brother. I'm not asking that.'

'This isn't about you,' says Ben.

He removes his glasses to rub his eyes, almost grinding them down, as he gathers and sorts his indignation.

'What do you want me to do, sit shiva for him? For Frank? Frank had a sick mind, a wicked heart. He can die. I don't have any pity for him. I don't have anything I need to tell him.'

'What does Beth say?'

'Beth? What else would she say? My wife is Jewish, born of a Jewish mother and a Jewish father, who themselves were born of Jewish parents – what do you think she would say?'

Ben crunches his hands into fists and takes a step toward his brother. Paul knew he would strike a nerve by mentioning his sister-in-law, but the reaction surprises him; his own body tenses instinctively. Ben comes no closer. Instead he places one hand on his chest and closes his eyes. With great effort, he hauls in a long breath.

'Are you all right?' asks Paul.

He watches as Ben lowers himself into the protective palm of an armchair. It's a frightening sight. He's accustomed to thinking of his older brother as invincible, the stone he cannot move. Ben breathes deeply as he regains his composure.

'It's my heart. I'm not supposed to get agitated.'

'Jesus, Ben.'

'Just give me a minute.'

Paul goes to the window. The bare trees of Central Park are collected in emaciated bunches around the dead lawns and their gray crusts of snow. Flakes of snow dance in the wind like gnats. He turns at the sound of his brother's voice.

'I'm not a kid anymore. A year ago I had a little hiccup, and since then it's been doctor's orders. I've been vigilant for salt, fat, sugar, caffeine. I read nutrition labels. I've renounced the poisons that make food worth eating. But my life isn't in any danger, as far as I know. I'll be here when Jake graduates from college, I'll be here to look after my wife when she's old. Do you understand that? I'm not going to fuck it up by letting Frank stick a monkey wrench in my heart. And I'm sure as hell not going to let you do it. You can come see me again, or not. It doesn't really matter to me which. But not until he dies. I know you're my brother, but sometimes that's just a word.'

Ben kneads his temples. His face is screwed into an expression of agony. Gray light fills the room.

'We haven't even talked about the will.'

'That my lawyer can handle.'

'Ben, be reasonable.'

'Am I not being reasonable? Then let me at least be clear. Unless he is dust and bones, don't come here again.'

Paul takes the train to the hospital in Fort Greene. He has a paperback, but glances away every few sentences to rifle through the incoming faces. He notices a woman, not quite his own age, who seems much more absorbed in her own book. When she turns the page he catches sight of the title: it's one he's read, but years ago, and he doesn't remember it well. She turns another page, and Paul studies her fingers – no ring. Unexpectedly, she looks up; she holds his gaze, a little defiant, but not resistant. The aluminum handlebar pounds in his grip as the train roars across a rough patch of track. Her eyes suggest solitude, a desire for novelty. She smiles briefly and goes back to her book. Paul returns the smile, too late for her to see. At one time he might have been able to make use of such an opening; he might once have had the energy. When the train pulls into the next station, he loses sight of her as a fresh assortment of passengers troops aboard. Soon after, his own stop arrives.

His father's body has been made strange by its diminishment; skin bunches awkwardly at the elbows and makes Paul think of the paper on a gift a child wraps for his mother. Machines do most of his breathing, and it takes long minutes of staring in silence to be convinced that his father's chest moves at all. If you pick up his arm, as Paul did, once, when the nurse was out of the room, it falls back to the bed without the slightest sign of struggle. They say his father is alive, but what's alive about him? He can't even express disgust at his own condition.

The doctors and nurses, who come and go in daily expectation of death, tell him to speak to his father. They say he can hear. Paul doesn't believe them and hasn't tried. He suspects the advice is for his own well-being, not his father's. Funerals, too, are for the living. He dislikes such pieties. When his father was in good health they spoke rarely; Paul knew him as a locked trunk whose contents revealed themselves by no more than the occasional rattle and scrape. It isn't that he wouldn't like to speak to his father. Childless at thirty-six, Paul now has an even greater curiosity, one that rises almost to anxiety, to know the man who raised him, or sporadically made the gestures of raising him – who was, at least, there. Above all to understand the man his father was in his youth, to hear him speak in the past tense. 'I thought' or 'I felt'; 'I wanted'; 'I believed.'

A nurse appears. She nods at Paul, the minimum gesture, and begins to check the machines.

'What do they tell you?'

She glances up from her clipboard.

'These machines.'

'Your father's vital signs, that's all. His blood pressure and pulse, his temperature.'

'His brain?'

'It's functioning.'

'How can you be certain?'

'If you put a light in his eye, his pupil responds.'

She purses her lips and returns to her ministrations.

'Do you know who my father is?'

She doesn't, of course – no one does any longer. The nurse stares again at the man in the bed, as if to see something she hasn't yet, perhaps cycling through a mental list of minor television actors and local politicians. Paul tries to decide if he will tell her. Even the barest facts would make her face go hard and her body snap tight. It isn't the sort of thing one explains casually. When she's certain she has no idea who he might be, other than Frank Metzger, a patient in the hospital where she works, one of the many dried-out bodies lying here to record the final ragged beats of their hearts, her eyes come back to Paul and ask, as they must, one question: *Who?*

Ten months into the lease and he can almost say he's used to the place: its speckled, run-down bathroom, the loose fixtures in the kitchen, the odd configuration which, like many prewar Brooklyn apartments, has been harshly renovated, indifferently carved and divvied to create as many units as possible within a single building. Its abiding virtue is price. Paul could find nothing cheaper. He knows and can mostly ignore its idiosyncrasies. The radiators, for instance. In winter they hiss like deflating tires, and the air feels like an extra layer of clothing. At least the place is tidy. One benefit of having few possessions is that clutter is nearly impossible. He wasn't always like this. In the last months, living again on his own has among other side effects disciplined him. Very few objects here have a history. There are his books, but, apart from an old coffee mug or the odd souvenir, the things he owns wouldn't tell a visitor much about him. The walls are bare.

On an end table he finds a single wineglass, in which swim the tepid dregs of last night's bottle — red and cheap — consumed in the company of a book and a recording of a Thelonius Monk concert purchased earlier that day, something they found in a library basement and remastered. He remembers thinking, around midnight, as alcohol and boredom were carrying him off to sleep, that he should take the trouble to wash the glass. Paul, stripping off his jacket, now makes a point of plucking it up by the stem and taking it to the kitchen, where, bent over the sink, he sponges the fingerprints from its fat underbelly.

Next he goes to the small office. It is meant to be the bedroom, but Paul, who sleeps on the pullout sofa in the living room, hasn't ever used it as such. He hears shouts and looks out the window. The snow has stopped. Some tall, rangy boys, a mix of ages and ethnicities bang around a soccer ball in the empty street. They scramble and taunt. Whites are moving into the neighborhood, prices are climbing, but as the avenue along the park bends and slopes southward from Windsor Terrace the families — Latin American, Southeast Asian, Middle Eastern, Chinese — still illustrate a larger atlas.

He watches until they are gone, as the bump and scrape of ball and pavement diminish, then vanish altogether. Their ease of movement has made Paul conscious of his own body, his thirty-six years. He's fine, he's in good shape, a lean six feet; he has all his hair. But he hasn't been inside a gym since his twenties, and for years the hair has been fading, like something exhausted, to an early gray. The difference is within. Paul has begun to sense the limits of his own life, a claustrophobia of aging: he feels trapped inside a failing piece of equipment. Routine physical effort — a flight of stairs, a heavy box — can now leave him short of breath. He can't locate when the change occurred, when his body first betrayed him. All he knows is that he can't do what these teenagers do.

On the roll-top desk in the office is a shambolic still life: pencils, pens, a broken watch, paper clips, a laptop computer, books, a calendar open to the wrong month, a lamp, paper, photographs, dust. This is the one zone of permitted disorder in the apartment. He moves a pile of books from the chair. In one of the drawers — he pretends not to remember which — are the pages of half a novel, something he was working on in his spare time last year. It was one of the few things Paul made a point of bringing with him when he moved, but he rarely thinks about it now. Lately he's had steady work, but as always he has to worry that it won't last. Editors are less generous than they used to be. He gets by. The articles come and go in a blur; it is difficult to recall the details of a thousand-word piece he submitted last month. Paul sits, retrieves a pen, seesaws it between his fingers. He stands again — there's no use pretending he's going to get anything done — and replaces the books on the chair.

In the living room he switches on the TV and turns it to one of the news stations. Another report on the rioting that has erupted overseas in protest of some cartoons in a Danish newspaper mocking Islam. It has been more than a month, and the demonstrations have only grown fiercer. People are dead. Muslims are inadvertently killing other Muslims while defending their prophet, incidental casualties during hazy, violent episodes of unrest. Every day Paul sees more images of clenched wild faces, flaming cars. It fascinates and horrifies him. He has put down a few thoughts on the subject, none of which has clotted into something he likes, and he's even mentioned the idea to a few editors. No one bit.

A reporter talks over footage of a rippling crowd. They scream in Arabic, Farsi; Paul wouldn't know. Protestors have called for the artists' heads. They alarm him even more than the advertised terrorists, the suicide bombers and sleeper cells. Terrorism, like road accidents and pickpockets on the subway, has become part of the basic weather of living. What he perceives as the roots of extremism — humiliation and hopelessness — make sense, in a way. But these protestors are ordinary men. They are unschooled in radicalism and otherwise not inclined to want murder. Some childish drawings have spurred them to demand it. Whatever name one prefers to give the turn of global events in the last five years — perhaps it is already a world war — it certainly hasn't ended. He was certain of that last year when London was attacked. Then Egypt. And now every conflagration — Iraq, Afghanistan, car bombs, soldiers, martyrs, beheadings, vandalized mosques and collateral damage, nightclubs and train cars ripped apart by explosives — the growing list of cities terrorized and disfigured — all of it has been reduced to a handful of childish drawings, a set of competing ideas: on the one side, a belief that some things do not belong to the corporeal world, to something as mundane as pen and paper, as coarse as human laughter; and, on the other, the principle that there is nothing which cannot be thought, printed, ridiculed.

Daylight has relented by the time he leaves the apartment again, and evening spreads above the city like a bruise. Paul's thoughts turn to his father's will. Naming him the sole beneficiary, it was signed only in the presence of a caretaker whose English is poor, and his brother's lawyer has pressed for a previous draft to be recognized, one that leaves Ben with fully three-quarters of their father's estate, including the payout on the life insurance. That version is decades old. Paul has no idea why his father waited so long to revise it; somehow he must have clung to the dismal hope that he and his firstborn son would be reconciled. Ben was never going to do that, and, although he must have his reasons for contesting the will, Paul doesn't understand. Ben is rich. He hardly needs what amounts to a modest inheritance. Paul has grown tired of fighting him – a fight that until this morning has been conducted solely through lawyers and the postal service. But he has no choice. It's money, and he's desperate. Frank Metzger will be dead by the end of the week.

Paul shouldn't even go out again. He's exhausted. Before getting on the subway he stops at the cafe by the station. It is an ordinary coffeehouse, with thatch-backed chairs and iron-legged tables, and in the heart of the afternoon it fills with young people on laptops and old men reading newspapers. By now they're gone, and the cafe is a vacant cube of light on the dark corner. He sees that a man he knows, Pirro, is working tonight. In the wicker baskets behind the glass counter, the day's last muffins and croissants nestle in blond heaps, like litters of sleeping puppies. They have a waxy, inedible sheen. Pirro, a Bosnian, is perhaps a few years younger than Paul, and his face – round, sunken, and fleshy – wears a carpet of stubble. Since moving to the neighborhood Paul has probably spoken to no one as often as Pirro. He sees him sometimes twice a day.

With his big hands Pirro wrestles the cash register and hits Paul with a fusillade of curses as soon as the door opens.

'What's the matter?'

'Oh – Paul. Good evening. It is nothing, just the fucking printer. It prints receipts that are nonsense.'

Still prying at the machine, he says, 'Have you heard what

the mayor wants to do? Charging cars to drive in Manhattan. Next they are going to make us pay to breathe the air. You want just a coffee?'

'I don't think it's such a bad idea. It will be good for the environment. It will be easier to get around.'

'Medium? My cousin runs a business. They drive trucks everywhere. Do you know how much this will cost him?'

'Medium's fine. They can use the money to repair roads, make the subways better.'

'Okay, let's see if the subway gets any better.' He seals the lid on the coffee. 'You shouldn't believe everything the mayor says, my friend.'

Paul laughs. As he's pulling out his wallet, Pirro waves a hand. 'Not tonight, my friend. On the house.'

'That's very kind of you.' The coffee is still too hot to drink and smells burnt.

'Now if I can just get this machine to work, we will really have reason to thank God.'

Paul waves as the door shuts after him. On his way to the subway he passes a group of men standing outside the corner bar, smoking cigarettes and, from the sound of it, already drunk. His mind elsewhere, he narrowly avoids walking into a fire hydrant and stumbles slightly, spilling some coffee. 'Careful!' cries one of the men as they all laugh.

The day's final errand brings him once more to Manhattan. He knows the address, an apartment south of Union Square, but hasn't seen the building, and the meeting is an unscheduled one – a half-formed idea, really, which has sat within him all day, and upon which, until now, it has been unclear if he would act. When he leaves the station it is even colder; he walks quickly, the digestive murmur of trains dying away behind him, even as his nerve for the endeavor starts to wane. He makes the turn onto the street he wants, passing the fogged, noisy windows of another bar, and when he finds her name next to the apartment number he feels a miserable, sickening turbulence. For a moment he studies the handwritten name like a piece of evidence.

He presses the bell.

'Hello?'

The hour is too late for a delivery, and her voice comes down the intercom's staticky chute pinched with anxiety. She isn't expecting anyone, then, although the possibility that she might have been occurs to Paul only now that he's at her doorstep.

'What are you doing here?' she asks once he announces himself.

'I have to talk to you.'

'You could have called.'

'It's my father. He's dying.'

She says, 'Hold on,' but the lock doesn't open. He waits. When she appears a few moments later it is apparent that she has already made up her mind about the distance to keep between them, about the expression to wear. She stands a few feet away and says nothing.

'I can't come up?'

They both watch the white curl of his breath expire in the air.

He knew the sight of his wife after so many months would affect him, but he couldn't have anticipated the hot, gluey pressure in his chest, the unceasing flap of blood down through his legs. They have spoken infrequently since the divorce, and this is the first time he has seen her face. He makes an inventory, beginning with the hazel eyes, then the drawn-down cheeks, the parentheses of sleek, dark hair; her thin lips part to expose a slash of perfect white teeth. She's always been beautiful. Everything is where it should be. Yet something, as present as the friction of clothes on skin, has changed.

As if reading his mind, she says, 'You look different.'

'Do I?'

She turns away, a private thought. He read once that when a person momentarily glances away before speaking, the direction of the glance distinguishes a recollection of fact from the invention of a lie, but Paul can't remember which is indicated by a turn to the left and which by a turn to the right; he gives up and instead lets his eyes trace the long asymptote of Claire's neck to where it vanishes beneath the line of her coat.

'This is why I didn't want to see you,' she says. 'Your face doesn't quite look right. I didn't want to know that I've started to forget what you look like.'

She's exaggerating, he knows, she too is addled, but her words nevertheless flood Paul with dreary imagination. Could she have walked by him without noticing? On a half-crowded street at noon, her mind divided between her starting point and her destination, preoccupied with other thoughts — of course she could have. What will survive of them? The day will come when they are strangers again, but less even than that: they will be strangers without the usual privileges of meeting for the first time — of a chance encounter, of newfound attraction. Of unexpectedly falling in love.

They go around the corner to a diner. Painfully bright fluorescent lamps glaze the faces of the few, solitary men who roost in the farther booths, huddled silently over plates of food they seem never to touch. Paul and Claire order coffees; she calls back the waitress and asks for a bowl of fruit.

'When did you last see him?'

'This afternoon. He's been unconscious for a week. He's got those tubes in his nose and machines are doing all the work. It's getting difficult to think of him as a person.'

'Paul. I'm so sorry.'

'There isn't a lot to be sorry about, you know that. Anyway, you never liked him.'

'Only because you told me not to. Before I'd even met him you put it in my head that this was a man people didn't like. Someone people hated. What else was I going to think? I was so young then.'

The waitress returns, sets down the chattering porcelain.

'You were twenty-six when we got married, Claire.'

She tears a grape from its stem. 'I hate it when you use my name like it's a slur.'

They take sips of coffee as the silence stretches out. A second couple comes in and occupies a nearby table. Paul tries to listen to their conversation but can hear only the scribble of voices.

'I didn't mean it that way,' he says finally. 'It's hard, seeing you after so long.'

'You're the one who came.' She's eating around the strawberries, which means she's saving them for last.

'Are you saying we're never supposed to see each other?' When she makes no response, he adds: 'We were married, Claire.'

She continues to drink her coffee and looks out the window. 'I'm just saying I don't know how long it would have been. I don't know what I'm supposed to think about you.'

'Then you do think about me.'

'As you say, we were married.'

Paul holds his breath. Looking through the window, he tries to find what might have caught her attention. He speaks next without turning, addressing her reflection.

'Are you seeing someone?'

'Is that what you came here to ask me?'

'No.'

'Then please, don't.'

He notices that she doesn't ask the same of him, then

realizes that by the tone of his question, by his insistence on asking it, he's already given her the answer. From her purse she takes a pack of cigarettes – this is new; she wasn't a smoker – and places it on the table.

'Are you still working on that book?' Claire spins the pack once. 'Forget it,' she says when he doesn't respond.

Two teenagers appear in the window. They saunter with a purposeless boredom, crisscrossing the street and hooting to each other in carelessly loud voices when they land on opposite sides. Draped in dark clothing, they gutter and flinch like smoke from a candle. Before they vanish around a corner, one coils his leg and, with a snap of muscle, kicks over a metal newspaper box. It crashes to the sidewalk and the noise flies into the windowpane. A single flag of newsprint shoots up like something sucked out of a fire. The boys don't look back. Paul turns to Claire, but she's slow to relinquish the scene, even though her face exhibits only a faint interest in what just happened. When at last she returns his stare, her eyes flash and she jostles her eyebrows at him.

'Look,' she says, 'if you're going to sit there staring at me like that, I don't see the point.' Something, perhaps an awareness of how cold those words are, catches her, and her eyes fill. 'This is a familiar silence.'

It draws out, the silence, as she regains control of her face.

Paul says, 'What about you? How are you?'

'I'm fine.'

'The job?'

'It's good. It's really good.'

A little current of tenderness washes through him. She means it, she is happy. Within a month of the divorce, she was hired onto the staff of one of the city's most famous art museums, after years of working in galleries. Were a man the source of this happiness, or even some other private, newfound joy, the warmth within him would be a bruise, a hemorrhage. But it is her work, and he knows how much it matters to her, he was present for its arc across those four, almost five, years — it's his life, too. 'I'm glad,' he says.

'Thanks. Thank you.' She smiles briefly, takes a sip of her coffee, and plunges her fork into the bowl of fruit. A grape. Carelessly she pierces it with her front teeth, and the plump red bead, as fat as an acorn, bursts in half, spraying juice across her chin; she unfolds a napkin. Then she looks at him and asks: 'Is everything arranged?'

Paul isn't thinking about his father; his brain reluctantly adjusts. 'I'm meeting with the funeral director tomorrow.'

He'd come here under the notion that he would ask Claire to accompany him to the funeral. Seeing her now, talking like this, he no longer wants to make the request, not only because he is sure the answer would be no, but because he doesn't want to let his father intrude and choke the fragile affection that has — he's not sure how — fluttered up between them.

'I am sorry, you know. He is your father.'

'I know.'

Acting on an impulse, he reaches out to snatch away a last glint of grape juice from Claire's cheek, then dries it against the sleeve of his jacket, and only afterward is he surprised that she didn't raise a hand to stop him. They talk a while longer, not really about anything; the couple behind them leaves. Then, with uncharacteristic suddenness, Claire stands and takes a cigarette from the pack with a thoughtless economy that tells him it's more than an occasional habit.

'I want to smoke this. Will you get the check?'

They return to Claire's building in silence. The area's usual noise is muted by the cold — a flinty, iron cold — that drives everybody indoors; each faceless building adds its silence to their own. At this moment, as at many others during their relationship, Paul gropes clumsily through his thoughts, looking for a phrase, a plea that will make his wife respond in some way – by a word, a gesture, a touch. Of the two, he walks more slowly. He is only partly conscious of making an effort to extend their time together. He has nothing to say; he isn't sure what he's allowed to say. He looks around: the black within black of a cat in an unlit window; paper at the top of an open trash can stirring like surf; the cement tattooed with cigarettes and lottery tickets. When they arrive he asks when he will see her again.

'I don't know,' she says. 'I haven't been your wife for a year.'

'Ten months,' he corrects her.

Wanting to say more, he stops himself, stung by how the rules have changed. There was a time when this tension would have matured into a real fight, the entire drama of shouting, doors slammed into silent halls – and then in the taut, trembling aftermath would come the tenderness of reconciliation, the mild kisses blossoming into full, gasping sex. The intensity of their arguments came from a powerful and mutual want: Paul wanted Claire to be different, just by a little, and she wanted the same of him. They had a good reason for wanting this – they did not want to be apart. Once, at the end of a fight, or perhaps at its beginning, she called theirs a relationship of ninety percent – ninety percent was good, it worked, and only the last ten percent didn't fit. He understood what she meant, but quibbled petulantly with the math; couldn't it be ninety-five or even ninety-eight percent? In this way, like all couples, they had arguments about their arguments. Tonight it's hard to imagine Claire raising her voice at all. Her only setting seems to be an exhausted tolerance.

Her eyes sink through him. 'Paul, Paul, Paul,' she says.

He isn't dressed to stand in the cold, and his ears sting, hot and numb at once. But he doesn't move. He doesn't want to lose what little he can say he has: this moment now, the memory of the last hour: her words and his, the flickering of her face, the uncontrived delicacy of her hands and the way they use the air. Two months ago she sent him an email. *I wanted you to know*, it said. She's Claire Brennan again; Claire Metzger has ceased to exist. The explanation was much longer, of course — it bulged with apology, guilt, pity, self-pity, and accusation — and, after he had read through it a second time, more calmly, he then calmly deleted it. He now recalls only its single noteworthy detail. It has been a point of minor obsession, in fact. One by one, the people with whom he shares a name are vanishing.

She is standing in the open door, and her face wears a curious, half-hearted expression. Some words shuffle up to his lips, since it seems to be his responsibility to speak, to release her back to this new life, but before he can do so he hears the words he might have wished for if he had thought there was any hope of hearing them: 'I guess you may as well come up.'

There's a problem with the trains. Paul's usual line isn't running properly between Manhattan and Brooklyn, and, like all city-dwellers, he takes it personally. Tonight the disruption is all the more excruciating because, in the limbo of a station where arrivals and departures are as rare as comets, there is nothing to guard him from his thoughts. Shortly after eleven, Claire asked him to leave. She didn't say why, but then again she didn't explain what inner swerve led her to ask him up in the first place. In the embarrassing aftermath he dressed hastily, aware that his nakedness had suddenly become a stain, a trespass; all told, he couldn't have been in her apartment for more than an hour. Only her bedroom, really, and the lights were out; he didn't even use the bathroom. Paul doesn't feel like a man who got what he wanted, even though, before she upended him with the invitation, he would have said there was nothing in the world he'd rather have.

Midnight has come and gone. He emerges from his stop trailing a group of three people, two men and a woman, whose conversation concerns a bar they want to find. It's a Sunday night, thinks Paul. But their enthusiasm appears unconditional. They are young, and perhaps, like him, have unconventional jobs, no place they belong in the morning. He feels empty, absent, dry, and, as they go in the opposite direction and their chatter shrinks to a papery crackle behind him, he walks toward home, mildly appalled by the idea of other people, of the claims company would make on him. He doesn't want to think. He wants only the privacy of sleep.

One block from the turn onto his street he hears the growl and bark of a new mix of voices, loud ones. Ribbons of laughter snap at the air. It is exceedingly rare to find people on his street at this hour, and he's still too far away to tell how many they are, but the speech has a shrill, excited quality; from a distance joy can sound like terror.

He makes the turn and sees them, stationed away from the ungainly glare of the streetlamp and — inevitably, he thinks — in front of his own building. Two stand, hurling back violent swallows from bottles sheathed in paper bags, and a third man, helpless from the load of alcohol in his body, is already on his knees, his arms chasing wildly around his head. Annoyed in advance at whatever idiocies they will heckle him with as he passes, Paul quickens his pace and sets his face in an uninviting scowl. He straightens his back, as if his posture alone can articulate his unwillingness to engage even in brief, good-hearted banter with these drunks.

He sees the two upright men splash liquor onto their friend. Christ, that's too much. Can they even feel how cold it is? Something is said – to Paul's ears it sounds like *Drink soma*, whatever that means – and again they all laugh. Though he is more than a block from his door, he digs around for his keys, wanting to get indoors as easily as he can. Not until he's close enough to see their faces does Paul realize that he has misread the scene. The man on his knees isn't laughing; he's silent, his face alert with fear, and he isn't a man at all, just a boy, perhaps sixteen or seventeen. He's maybe Middle Eastern or South Asian. He could be one of the kids Paul saw earlier playing soccer in the street. When again one of the men speaks, following another dousing from the bottle, the words are clear: 'Drink, Osama.'

Paul hesitates only briefly, then starts to walk directly toward them. Without a clue as to how such an episode materialized on his block, he understands that he has to intercede, and imagines that as soon as they realize they aren't alone the two louts will clear out.

He is too late. Before reaching them he watches in horror as the boy is forced to the ground from behind; there's no mistaking the fleshy clap of face and pavement. No one moves to help him up. Then, with two long strides, one of them administers a punishing kick to the ribs. At the sight Paul's hands strangle the fabric inside the pockets of his coat. Nerves scream. They want him to do the sensible thing, the selfish thing – to run away. A vague principle holds cowardice in check. The fear of shame prevails. Men don't run.

Paul has never been in a fight. Something shivers inside him, an alien energy that takes control of his actions, and, without being fully conscious of doing so, he searches himself for a weapon. There are the keys, whose touch and innocent chime seem too ordinary, too domestic. But he has nothing else. His fingers, looking for a sensible way to hold them, play with the keys. He chooses one and closes his hand around it; it nestles between the middle and ring fingers, a good fit. The firmness of the metal calms him somewhat: the key's teeth feel convincing. A startling image surfaces unbidden: throwing a punch and tearing a hole in someone's cheek. Nothing like this has ever occurred to him, yet it is solid and familiar, as if it has always been there, this immediate and unexpected resourcefulness, an idea locked in the genes.

He stops. Ten feet separate him from them. He's been seen.

No one speaks. The men, who are white with hair cut close to the scalp and dress identically in black leather jackets, stand a bit awkwardly, like actors onstage who have forgotten their lines. Yet nothing about them indicates a trace of concern or panic—he isn't a policeman, he hasn't any visible claim to authority. Tattoos of intricate, spidery black grip the base of each man's throat, crawling upward, almost to the hinge of the jawbone. The boy, twisted and limp and tangled around himself like wet cloth, is still in too much pain to rise. Spots of blood pepper the concrete; the violence didn't begin with Paul's arrival. The boy's nose is a mess. Both men wear the surly, dull expressions of the uneducated, and both are considerably younger than Paul—twenty-two, twenty-three. He reminds himself that he is calm.

Sensing that someone has to break the silence, he says, 'I think he's had enough.' Meanwhile he sizes them up. Is it only sport to them, a flare-up of spontaneous drunken aggression, or has Paul stumbled onto something much darker, a premeditated assault, a sick idea of American justice? The boy's race can't be an accident.

'Who the fuck are you?'

This response comes from the shorter of the two, who, though he stands farther from Paul, projects the greater menace. His eyes drift from alcohol, perhaps also from the drugged aftermath of violence, yet they communicate a sharpness, a stability and assurance that suggest he won't be knocked aside just because he's drunk, just because he lacks Paul's advantages in age, education, and status.

'Look. Why don't you just go and leave him with me? I live right here. I'll make sure he gets home. We can all forget this ever happened.'

He has offered an exit, a way to save face, by suggesting that they've proved their point, which feels like a betrayal of principle: it concedes that they have a point, that until now their actions have been perfectly reasonable. It makes him complicit, somehow. Under the close-cut cap of pale hair, almost white in this light, the man's face makes an expression of mild amusement. Paul would have preferred to issue a stronger, a categorical, denunciation, not to surrender to the terror mounting within him. But it is there, terror, and it isn't going away. Nor are they.

'He's just a kid,' Paul says, directing his words at the presumed leader. He adds, as an afterthought: 'Someone has certainly called the police by now. You're making an awful lot of noise. I could hear you three blocks away.'

They make no response. With each subsequent statement, each new effort to reason with these men, he senses the mounting futility of it; at each word they are more rooted to the spot, more invested in their brutal act. Something in his chest swells, as if his body is suddenly too small to contain what's inside. Sweat stipples the skin of his face even in the cold, and because of the cold it stings; but inside he is hot, and hurricanes of blood churn between his bones and spin out to the ends of his arms.

The nearer man looks back for instruction and at this cue

his partner, clearly the author of this event, opens his mouth at first merely to grin, knotting up the skin of his face like a gargoyle's, and then, with a great smoky breath, he laughs. Soon they're both laughing, these two men, whose white faces emerge vividly from the night behind them.

Through the laughter one of them says, 'Man, don't be an idiot — fuck off,' and everything begins to happen very quickly: something surges through Paul like electricity: the key feels hot in his hand, tight between the knuckles. Talk is useless. He throws a punch at the near man, and though it lands on target he didn't set his feet, he's off balance, and the motion feels horribly unnatural, an imitation of something he once saw. It has the desired effect — the man staggers back — but the other is already closing in. He attempts another crooked punch and this time pays the price: his grip on the key loosens. The man's jaw pushes it back into his hand, and the whole key chain falls to the sidewalk with a weak splash.

First the one, and then both, attack him. He doesn't know how many times he's struck, as his consciousness telescopes away from his senses, the hard, dull blows railing his body from front and back and accumulating in a flat, wooden pain that spreads through his side, under his ribs, warm and uneven; his legs buckle, the sky tilts swiftly away from him at a fierce angle, and the sidewalk flies up to receive the back of his skull. Even his mouth registers the impact — a zinc flavor coating his tongue from root to tip, a flavor like the admission of defeat. For an instant his mind closes, everything shutting down, turning to black. He's aware only of the pavement beneath him, the distinct unnatural feeling of lying on a plane of such hard stuff. Above him the men's voices are muffled.

'Who is he?'

'He's a dumb fuck, that's what he is.'

Paul's head clears, and they sense it; they look down. A moment passes in which nothing happens, a slice of possibility: they may be content with just this, Paul lying on the ground and humiliated but without serious injury. He waits. One of the two men — the leader, he's certain of it — comes toward him, and before Paul can trace the path of the boot he feels it in his ribs, a sharp wedge of pain, the impact ringing through stiff limbs. He feels terribly fragile; his fingertips feel hollow. Almost immediately, the man delivers another kick of the same force and trajectory, and with a groan Paul rolls away, onto his other side.

No one's in a hurry to leave; they laugh. The men have settled in once more, adapting to the idea of distributing their violence across two victims instead of just the one. They have ugly faces, with heavy jaws and cheeks blasted red by the weather, full of bleak brutality. Maybe this began as an idle amusement, but it has become a piece of business that must be brought to an end.

They are rolling Paul onto his back, almost coddling him, treating him for the moment like the injured creature he is. This is new to him, the grammar of violence, these small intermissions used to emphasize the cruelty. His bones ache. Do they plan now to kill him? He is defenseless; the muscles in his legs flatten on the ground like wet sand. The chance remains that these men know a boundary. Even in the haze of drink and violence they may still respect the bright line between beating a man and killing him. There's no telling. Then the leader, with the menace legible on his face, lifts his leg and clamps a boot firmly down on Paul's neck.

One good push would do it — crush his windpipe, put an end to everything. The man doesn't give it. Not yet. Paul summons the strength to lift his arms and take hold of the man's ankle, but he can't do much from this position and makes no effort to throw off the leg; the determination isn't there. Instead he merely holds it, like a child clinging with both hands to his mother's arm.

'How's that? Comfortable?'

The man's speech is self-consciously tough: his words are part of the posture he uses to keep his lieutenant in line.

'You cut my friend. Don't you see what you did to him?'

'Didn't you hear him? Terence told you look at my face.'

But he can't: no part of him can move. He hears the metallic rip of a zipper's teeth and then the gentle cackle of urine splashing on pavement. His nose fills with its warm, animal smell.

'Maybe he's sorry now. Are you? Are you sorry for trying to help your terrorist friend?'

He begins to increase the pressure on Paul's neck. Bright, urgent flashes appear at the edges of his vision. He pushes his nails into the man's legs but through thick denim the gesture is meaningless. The pissing stops, and the voices above him grow faint. He gurgles.

Glass shatters near his ear. The other man has dropped his bottle only inches from Paul's face. The crude aroma of malt liquor mixes with the urine and swims into his nose while his hands rattle the ankle like a broken doorknob before falling away to flop pointlessly against the rough asphalt. As he floats closer to darkness, the back of his hand brushes something unexpected, a quick, light prick. Pain has become a single idea — the weight of the boot — and to discover it elsewhere is startling, perverse. His hand turns to examine the object: smooth, cold, and deeply curved in the middle, like a shell. Glass from the broken bottle. Paul scoops it into his fingers and brings his hands back around the man's ankle. This earns another smirk. He slips the glass between the fabric of the pants and the bare leg, inching up the long, inviting bulge of calf and then trowels it under the skin, using his thumb for leverage. He forces it in as far as he can and with all his remaining strength drags down. It sickens him, opening this gash in the man's leg: he doesn't use a sawing motion, as he would for tough meat, and the flexed muscle resists its passage; the irregular edge of the glass stutters through flesh, a dense, grisly tremble between his fingers, but he doesn't stop, even as he feels the opposite edge pierce his own skin, he ignores the pain, continuing to press and pull, even as he feels a warm dribble of blood.

Several things happen at once. The foot lifts from Paul as the man, howling, leaps and then staggers away. His accomplice, panicked and unsure what has happened, takes a few running steps from the scene, as if Paul has unleashed a hidden power. Air explodes into his lungs as he gasps and wrestles it in; a dry retch rises from his stomach. For a moment the leader looks unsure whether to follow his partner. Paul still lies on the ground, but he's proven to be less than ideal prey, capable of biting back. Then, as if suddenly realizing the extent of his injury, the man's face crumples in agony. At first he limps around, and then with a cramped, graceless haste he chases his friend into the darkness.

Paul groans. The pain in his throat begins immediately to diminish, though he still struggles to breathe. He coughs and spits, trying to evacuate the salty taste of blood, and then, as he sits up, a damp ache spreads across his back and shoulders. He places a hand on his ribs where he was kicked — nothing seems broken. Already he realizes what he has escaped. He won't even need to go to the hospital.

The boy is already on his feet. The moment does not have the sense of rushed camaraderie that shared traumas are said to bring about. Rather, the kid has a defensive, angled stance; tension constricts his battered face, a tender unrest upon the smooth features, a murmur in the skin. There's no gratitude in it. In the cold, the blood around his nose has already dried to a black crust, and he seems to be waiting for instruction from Paul. The adult. The samaritan. Paul does not feel any more certain of the appropriate course of action. It's the boy who fixes the point. He turns and, without a word, runs. In a matter of strides he sheds the punishment his body just endured. Paul hasn't got the energy to call after him and doesn't know what he would say if he did. He wonders what causes the boy to flee now, after the threat has passed, and then sees what might have done it: in his right hand he still holds the large shard of glass, and even in bad light it plainly shows the stains of its recent use.

2

By morning bruises have blossomed across his ribs. They have the sheen and deep color of rotting plums and hurt to the touch. The cuts on his hand weren't deep — scabs already cover them — but there is a long red welt on his throat, above the collar, which hasn't diminished at all. He worries that the man's boot broke something under the skin that will never heal.

It is Monday. Paul has a meeting with a book editor who contacted him about an unspecified project. He would prefer to remain in isolation, and feels an arthritic reluctance to rejoin the outside world. For an hour before leaving he sits in his apartment in a state of mental exhaustion; even to think he must contend with the massive headache which, rising up like an iceberg, greeted him almost at the instant of consciousness and split apart the watery half-dreams that flicker between sleep and waking. Last night's multiple events compete for a claim to his attention. Only hours ago he was pinned to the pavement, as close to death as he has ever come, although there's no way to know if they intended to go through with it — with killing him — or if they had already reached their threshold when his hand found the piece of glass. He was in such pain. Unaccustomed to violence, he perhaps wouldn't have known the difference between pain that kills and pain that doesn't. Regardless, he feels glad, almost proud, to have done it — to have located, in a time of need, this resourceful solution. Paul fondles the secret like a new acquisition, and from it, from this isolated incident framed safely in the past, he receives an unexpected, pleasurable jolt; momentarily he forgets Claire. His thoughts are tinged with a pale madness — he feels wild to have survived such a thing, and his heart boils in a residue of adrenaline. The sensation is like nothing he's ever known; he can sense in it an addictive strength. What raw, extraordinary violence his hands are capable of. It will be strange to resurface in a world that knows nothing of what happened.

He dresses, choosing a cream-colored shirt, sports coat, blue jeans, and unpolished brown shoes, an ensemble that Claire, with gentle condescension, used to call his writer's costume — even if, as she was quick to admit, she thought he looked handsome in it. It was one of their jokes. He stifles another memory of last night's pleasureless sex, of the vacant expression on Claire's face as he came, and finishes putting on his clothes. It's difficult, anyway, to remember what he would like to remember: the lights stayed off the whole time. Last week, on the phone, the editor — a man called Bentham — insisted that Paul would want to see him, but was stubbornly unforthcoming about what he had in mind. Paul imagines it must be ghostwriting, something of that sort. He stands at the bathroom mirror, playing with his collar, which, no matter how he adjusts it, doesn't conceal the dark welt on his neck. This meeting could mean work, yet he isn't looking forward to it, not because of nerves, but because conversation with a stranger, the recital of banalities, is a chore. He isn't used to it. His time is his, alone.

He surfaces in midtown, rising into the sudden crush of activity, the pageant of matching men and women, precisely dressed, who march against the wind — ties flapping, skirts pressed around knees — while jawing into mobile phones and tapping on small electronic screens. He walks quickly, crossing a square as pigeons the size of footballs waddle stupidly out of the way. There's no reason to hurry – he is in fact a little early for the meeting at Bentham's office, near the top of a forty-story tower on Madison Avenue. It looms suddenly as he turns onto the block. Stacked against the sky, such buildings reliably impress Paul, a testament to exactly the sort of ambition he does not possess: calling it greed is reductive, even though it's exactly the word he would once have used. Another of the conservative compromises of age, this lexical tempering, this revision of self. Ten o'clock. People step out for the first cigarette of the morning. Knotted in cliques of two and three, they speak in voices too low for Paul to hear.

Weekdays are strange. Fresh out of college he worked as a reporter but after three years decided that he preferred to be on his own. Since then Paul hasn't held a proper nine-to-five. His intention may once have been to chase a life that was more glamorous. He took a few stabs at writing a novel, including the one last year, but nothing ever came together in a way he liked, and before meeting Claire he left New York to do graduate study at the University of Chicago, reading for a thesis on the postwar Central European writers; it didn't pan out, and a year later he was back. With time these urges have grown small, then fallen away altogether. The life he's built for himself – modest, self-contained, and, yes, with a kind of freedom – makes the best use of his natural talents: he writes, editors solicit articles from him, and he's built a healthy catalog of bylines, even if a more enduring success has eluded him. His aspirations now have implicit bound-aries. He no longer feels – if indeed he ever really did – the gnaw of ambition, that desire for greatness that constrains some men like the iron rings of a wine cask. When money gets tight he takes jobs he wouldn't otherwise – copywriting, proofreading, freelance editing – but he reminds himself that it is a small price to live without a fixed place of business and have no one to whom he must answer.

The result of his lifestyle is that, when he steps into the street in the middle of the day, he feels foreign, even a little criminal. Adults are supposed to be at work, in offices, factories, fields; he isn't.

Bentham meets him just outside the elevator. He is shorter, older, and rounder than Paul, yet projects an energy his visitor cannot match. His collar is open. Stylish, wire-rimmed eyeglasses attest to an attention to the trimmings of his profession. He bounces a look off Paul's face as they shake hands.

'I was sorry to hear about your father's health.'

'You know my father?'

'Not personally,' says Bentham. 'Word gets around.'

He ushers Paul into his office, where the smell of expensive things – leather, cologne, high-quality paper – immediately pinches his nose. Nothing wears any age. On the desk stands a menagerie of emaciated metallic sculpture, arranged to articulate unassuming elegance, an impression further embellished by the subdued abstract art that hangs on the walls. Books line the shelves, as straight and neat as good teeth.

'Close shave?'

Paul doesn't at first understand that the question refers to the abrasion on his neck. He makes a vague remark about a fall on some ice; Bentham lets it drop. Instead he compliments him on an article he recently published in *New York* magazine on the long gestation of the proposed Second Avenue subway line; Paul listens without offering a reply. If Bentham believes that a small dose of such attention will impress him, he's misjudged his audience. Perhaps if Paul were accustomed even to a trickle of regular acclaim these days, his appetite for the stuff would be stronger; speaking to an actual reader of his has become so rare an event that praise has acquired a peculiar, not entirely pleasing flavor.

'Have you ever thought of doing a book?'

In reply Paul makes a gesture that says, *Who hasn't?*

'Any ideas at the moment?'

'Do you want to hear them?'

Bentham pauses, considering his next words. He smiles at Paul, a smile that is meant to be ingratiating, and asks: 'What do they pay you, Paul? How much for a word?'

He holds a neutral expression, makes no reply.

'Professional curiosity.'

Finally, deciding there's no harm in it, Paul mentions a number.

'How would you like to make a lot more than that?'

At first Paul simply laughs. Bentham doesn't smile. He is serious. Paul has, until this moment, been baffled as to what this man could have in mind, but now wonders how he missed it. 'You want me to write about my father.'

'Yes.'

'I won't.'

'Hear me out. This would be entirely your book, to take in whatever direction you'd like. The fact is, there are a lot of readers to be reached on the memoir shelf these days. I've done a little reading about your father. We think there's a market for your story.'

'My story's nothing.'

'Your father's, I mean.'

'How do you even know about it?'

'Your brother. I've been reading the articles; one of them mentioned your father. Frank Metzger. Nothing's been written about him for decades, it seems. I looked up a few things. He had quite a life. And of course I remembered your name. You're a talented writer. Maybe you just haven't had a big enough subject.'

Paul exhales sharply. 'I'm afraid you have the wrong idea. I was born in 1969. My father wasn't anybody then. Even if I were interested . . . everything you'd want me to write about, I wouldn't be able to. I wasn't even alive.'

'No one remembers your father, and I wouldn't have heard of him if it weren't for your brother's current — predicament. But it's a unique story, a great hook. It just needs a personal angle. What makes this a viable project is what you bring to it. You're the son. You've got the name.'

'You're asking the wrong person. I've got no interest, and, even if I had, I wouldn't know where to begin.'

'Paul. This could be a big book. You'd really say no to that?'

'I'm willing to.'

'Think of it as a chance to address his critics. To tell his — to tell *your* side of the story.'

'I'm not sure I have a side of the story.'

That smile again: like a leopard's.

'All I'm asking is that you think about it,' the editor says. 'Forget about the money for a minute. Think of what this does for you as a writer. You don't even have an agent. With this under your belt, all of a sudden you're getting more offers for magazine work than you know what to do with. You've got a second book on the way. Just think about it. It's all history now. The dead don't complain.'

Or the nearly dead, thinks Paul. He says, 'My father thought he was being a patriot. He wanted to be more important than he was, and he believed he was going to change history. He was young. He was misguided.'

'Most people would use stronger language than that.'

'I'm not trying to defend him. Look, it's difficult already, knowing the man he once was. I haven't got the slightest interest in dwelling on it any more than I already have.'

Bentham maintains an imperious detachment. He stands. Seeing him framed by the impressive office, by the material evidence of his profession and his taste, Paul feels outgunned. The refusals have done nothing to diminish Bentham's glow of assurance. One way or another, he clearly believes, Paul will see the logic of the offer.

'If you change your mind, call me,' says Bentham. 'I've even thought of a title.'

Curiosity gets the better of him; at the door he stops to look at Bentham. He waits. The editor lowers his voice.

'The American Nazi.'

In the elevator Paul feels an angry desire to expel from memory Bentham's last words. To spit them out. He hasn't got the luxury of silence and time to consider what has been asked of him, to sort through the annoyance and shame he feels. He is expected elsewhere, and quite soon – in the space of half an hour he must hurry back to the train, descend, switch lines, emerge again in Brooklyn, and then walk the several blocks to the funeral home that will manage the care of his father's body once it is beyond the help of doctors and nurses. He touches the welt on his neck, which is warm and has begun to itch. He's spoken once already with the mortician to arrange the business of his father's funeral. Questions concerning the expected number of guests proved especially difficult: there perhaps exist people of whom Paul is unaware and who have reason to come – but as far as he knows the number in attendance, besides himself, will be zero.

He walks as fast as he can. There are people to avoid, both the hard-walking businessmen and the oblivious tourists, there are trash cans, street vendors, mailboxes, parking meters. There are dog leashes stretched like trip wires, doors swinging suddenly open. Delivery boys on bicycles bounding onto the sidewalk. Lampposts and fat black garbage bags piled like dung heaps. But the mind is agile, annoyingly so, and it can perform its physical responsibilities, ushering the body through even a cluttered space while operating on other frequencies. It is the source of the will, but the will has little control over it. In direct affront to his staunch and bilious reaction to the editor, Paul, in the back of his mind, finds himself knocking together sentences and paragraphs: he is writing.

Frank Metzger, the son of German immigrants, was twenty-four when Hitler came to power. He was living by himself on the Lower East Side and working at a lawyer's office. His principal ambition was to become a poet. To date, however, that dream was more batter than cake; he thought about poetry much more than he actually wrote it. Up to this point, the story is a familiar one — an early, ill-defined wish for greatness that rattles around inside a young man.

The train arrives. Paul peruses the faces of other passengers and feels his thoughts recede. Across from him sits an elderly woman, already pushed against the back of her life — hair stretched tight by curlers, carefully dressed, somebody's grandmother. From a cavernous blue purse she pulls a thin, thumb-worn booklet titled *The Lord Hears Your Cries.* For twenty minutes, turning the pages with exaggerated delicacy, she recites from it, just under her breath, her lips moving rapidly, as if chewing on each word. She rarely blinks. Her eyes have a child's shine.

Prayer was once important to Paul. For his tenth or eleventh birthday, at an age when one finds tremendous joy in a plot if it offers up a good explanation of things, a friend's mother gave him a volume of children's stories from the Bible, and he was immediately receptive to the dramatic, occasionally gruesome fascination of those tales. He soon graduated to the real thing, whose dense bricks of type and obscure prose only increased its allure — a puzzle to be solved, an intellectual leap of greater, graver daring. He read, and read, and read. His eyes went sore. He was amazed at how full his head now was, at how full it had always been, and amazed that this fullness was completely private. He went warm when he thought of it. This faith was his, and he was newly free; he had found something that was not his father's, that was purely his own. Paul became a believer. He quickly adopted the habits of prayer and penitence, acclimating himself to the sudden reversals of emotion when, during a brief interlude of instinctual pleasure, guilt flew in to sting and infect it. Guilt was good because it wasn't random: it obeyed a set of principles, and with regulated, predictable behavior one could avoid it altogether.

In college Frank had studied history and philosophy, while growing increasingly intrigued by his German heritage, a fascination that dated back to the end of the Great War. His own father's emotions then had been mixed: though he loved his adopted country, the humiliation of Germany's defeat sank deep within him. Of his father's complicated emotions Frank had inherited only what his young mind could easily grasp — the disappointment.

His father's thoughts on faith were quite clear. When Paul first took up religion, Frank did not ignore the change in his son — in fact, the derision he showed was the most attentive he'd yet been as a parent. This flare-up of paternal interest declined once Frank grew bored with it, and, as a teenager, Paul put away his piety. With time it came to seem a puerile act of rebellion against a diminished, disinclined father. Faithlessness brightened within him like the lights at the end of a movie. Strangely, Paul began to recall his father's tirades almost with approbation; Frank was cruel, but he gave his son the truth. Paul came to feel slightly uncomfortable toward this younger self, and he even began to feel a sense of common cause with his father, another man who saw through the lie of belief. He would twist with mortification to remember that before going to sleep he often whispered, up into the darkness of his empty room, 'I love you.' In his life he's had little use for the tonics of therapy, but even he can see that he spoke those words to God because he had no one else to speak them to. He finally stopped because he was suffering from what later strengthened into outright embarrassment – he felt silly. As soon as he began to suspect that no one was listening, the prayers turned to salt in his mouth. His own father was miserly with affection and at times his presence barely registered – he seemed less an actual person than a concept, a climate within the house – but at least Paul knew, night after night, which room he slept in. God, it turned out, wasn't there at all.

As Hitler was consolidating his power, Frank fell in with the sons of other German immigrants and, in 1934, was introduced to some members of the German-American Bund. That summer he attended a rally at Madison Square Garden, which concentrated and gave shape to his new avocation. Within a year he was spending weekends at a camp on Long Island devoted to the glorification of the 'New Germany' and the promotion of German-American ties. It was there that he swore an oath to the Führer.

At the funeral parlor in Williamsburg an assistant greets Paul, and as she steers him through a series of corridors he can't help but notice that they avoid any brush with the reminders of mortality that must elsewhere fill the building. The weeping, the embalming, the cremation – those occupy other rooms. What he's allowed to see of the place brings to mind a dentist's office. Walls painted a stark, antiseptic white. Clean, well-lit hallways, plants standing in the corners, filing cabinets lined up and locked.

Frank rose rapidly through the hierarchy of the Bund, thrilled by the sense that he was part of something greater than himself and of something also that made him greater. He set up and ran the organization's official publication. Soon he was involved in the management of funds; one of the Bund's only material efforts in service of the Reich was to funnel American dollars into German coffers. He believed what they all believed. Germany and the United States would become partners, coequals, in a new world order; at rallies they flew the swastika alongside the stars and stripes. Frank stood at an extraordinary vantage. He was awash in the changing waters of history; when he moved, history moved with him. Here his linguistic talents served him well. His fame within the Bund soared. As a speaker of German he was mediocre, but when safely in his native tongue he was eloquent on the subject of greatest importance to those who gathered at Long Island: Germany as the inevitable phoenix, history's definitive and most glorious empire — the Reich of a thousand years.

As Paul enters the main office, the funeral director, whose name is Wolff, extends an arm.

'I am sorry about your father,' he says after the exchange of pleasantries. 'Rest assured, he's in good hands.'

The moment of greatest personal glory came for Frank when he took it upon himself to offer to the Nazis a special delivery of funds — his own. His father had left him a modest inheritance of three thousand dollars, which he took — in cash — to Berlin and donated to the Nazi Party. Inflation continued to erode Germany's economy; dollars were extremely valuable. He had expected a grander reception than the one he received. A bureaucrat accepted the money without emotion and made a note in a register. No handshake, no ceremony, no medal.

The mortician is younger than Paul expected. In his early forties, a widow's peak rising into a swipe of dark black hair above his angular face, Wolff leans back in a high leather chair with the studied ease of an executive. Paul is a tourist in these affairs of mortality. It's his father who will depart the known world, a man Wolff has never laid eyes on, but at the instant Frank Metzger ceases to be a human being and becomes only a body, he becomes Wolff's business. For him death is a practical rather than a philosophical riddle. Wolff is the one who's willing to put his fingers under the skin, the one who knows how to get a dead body into a suit; he's the one who fires up the cremator. One of his palms, Paul notices, lies carelessly open on the table between them, as if waiting for a coin.

'Do you have any siblings?'

'None,' says Paul.

'A wife?'

'No.'

'So it's only you. That's quite a burden for a son.'

Even in the wake of his disappointing reception in Berlin, Frank pursued the Bund's work with the blindness and the happiness of religious devotion. His fame continued to grow — in fact, it began to spill over into the wider world as word spread of the organization. On the eve of Hitler's invasion of Poland, prosecutors indicted several of the leadership at the Long Island camp. Frank wasn't among them. But because of his notoriety within the party, his was the face the newspapers ran to accompany the articles; at that age he had the kind of severe, slightly fussy handsomeness people expected of a Nazi. Later, in 1944, he was part of a group that was put on trial for sedition. Prosecutors alleged a widespread Nazi conspiracy to overthrow the American government. Newspapers across the country reported it, deriding Frank as little more than a dull pawn of his German handlers. He spent two months in prison, but in the end the charges against him and the others were dropped for lack of evidence.

'On the phone you said he was still in the hospital.'

'Yes. They expect him to—' Paul coughs. 'That is, any

day now.' He dislikes euphemism, but others seem to prefer it around death. 'My father doesn't have any friends, that I know of.' Not sure why he has made a point of saying this now, he decides to add, 'He and I aren't especially close.'

The mortician scratches his nose with his ring finger. It's bare. Paul finds it odd that this man isn't married; undertakers, like politicians, should have wives, conventional family arrangements.

'May I ask if you are still able to speak with him, Mr Metzger?'

'Call me Paul.'

'May I ask that, Paul?'

After the trial Frank left New York for Arizona — it meant going west, a new start. For two years he sold topsoil and fertilizer. He sulked, plotted, daydreamed. And he married his first wife, who knew nothing of his past. Then, only three years after departing, he returned to New York with bride and new son in tow. The Nuremberg trials and the continued unearthing of evidence about the death camps and the extent of the Nazis' crimes maintained interest in the villains of the war. Reporters knocked regularly on the door of their small house in Brooklyn. With time the interest died; the knocking stopped. Frank drifted back into the ordinary swim of humanity. Few people still recognized his name. The man whose picture had been splashed across newspapers faded behind history — his infamy wouldn't survive even for a generation.

'He can't speak, no. The doctors say it's possible he understands me when I talk to him, but I don't believe them.' Paul laughs. 'He looks dead. Only the machines believe he's not.'

There is an uneasy silence. Paul coughs again. At last the funeral director speaks.

'So often we look for an easy way through this, but there never is one.'

When Paul was in college the father of a close friend died unexpectedly. They have since lost touch, he and the friend, but he remembers the powerful feeling of watching someone endure that rite of passage. In the days that followed, his friend stood up to it — *like a man*, the words they used — even though he and his father were surely closer than Paul is with his. The event bestowed upon the friend an aura, a masculine gravity. His steadfastness became myth. There's none of that now. Fathers die.

'Is it possible to hold the service here?'

'We have a space, if that's what you wish.'

'My father wasn't a religious man. There's no reason to use a church.' Wolff's uninviting silence stops Paul before he can offer a further explanation. 'I'd like to see it, the room.'

'Of course,' says Wolff, rising.

His past was too much. He lost the wife, the son. She swore never to speak to her husband again, but from time to time, and with his mother's blessing, the boy, called Ben, visited — he was young and carried around a natural curiosity about his father. He arrived at Frank's door for the last time when he was seventeen, and then only to tell him that he had made up his mind to jettison the name Metzger. He wanted nothing to do with Frank's disgrace, a crime so great that, although he was not yet born at the time, he considered it unforgivable. He would make his way in the world as Ben Wald. He then, and ever, considered himself fatherless.

They travel the same channels that brought Paul to the director's office. Wolff turns right and opens a large set of white doors; in the room beyond there are no windows and the lights are off. Paul is the first to enter. For an instant he's alone. The awareness that this room, of all rooms, has hosted so much death, so much grief, puts Paul in a reverent mood: for a different man it might be a religious moment.

Faith – the manufacture of certainty in the dark. Behind him, he hears Wolff turn a switch, and then an insectlike hum as electricity pours into the old lamps.

'As you can see, we have everything you'll require,' says Wolff, but Paul only half listens. The room, now lit, is a drab affair. Chairs wait in military lines, their upholstery well-worn by so many mourners; paths of gnarled thread streak the carpet between the rows where the living walk, where restless shoes knead the floor during the recitation of the deceased's life. Everything's old, nothing like the modern style, the lucid precision, elsewhere in the building. Time has ground down the room, and it repulses Paul, the thought not of his father but of anybody spending his last day aboveground here.

'Most of our clients do choose to hold the service in a church,' says Wolff, as if sensing Paul's thoughts.

'This is fine.'

Later Frank remarried, a much younger woman, a secretary at the company where he'd found work. They had a son. But fatherhood was too much for him; marriage, too, was surely difficult, even though, only two years after the birth of their child, she died – in a car accident, with her lover, the first Frank knew of the affair. All the dreams of his earlier days, of poetry and eminence, were gone. He didn't write. Instead he sank into years and years of silence and isolation. After his younger son left for college he did not again share his home with another person.

Paul doesn't normally think of the Frank who swore an oath to Hitler. His own memories are of a man who even in good restaurants fished ice cubes out of the water glass because they hurt his teeth; who spoke little and slept late; who never had the stomach for anything stronger than beer. But those things don't matter, not to anyone else. The existence of a domestic self doesn't exculpate a man from his poor choices. To the wider world it means nothing that he could claim the qualities all fathers, all men, have. Bentham may be right: a book could sell. And it could even make use of such facts as these, but by themselves they aren't enough. Each detail would have to be cased in a thick rime, a reminder that – yes – Frank Metzger was a Nazi, too.

Wolff's voice breaks in. 'Will you desire a viewing of the body?'

'That won't be necessary. He wants to be cremated.'

The pain of his father's past has always been oblique, coming at him crabwise, sneaking in when he least expects it, because there isn't ever a moment when one expects to have such a man for a father. He's never made his peace with it. Most of the time he simply forgets about it. For Paul it doesn't have the piquant sting of lived experience, living memory; it is an inherited shame. It is a story. Even so, when something imposes the facts upon him, as this morning has, he can't stop thinking about it, worrying it, like a kid with fresh stitches.

Coming upon a man selling meat from a cart, he stops, aware that he's been walking quickly and without a destination. Cottony white steam pours from the grill, where heaps of shredded beef and chicken cook, mixed with onions and green peppers and caked in aromatic red spice. Saliva creeps under his tongue. Lately his eating habits have been sporadic, and he is suddenly, violently hungry; he orders a sandwich and then disposes of it in several bites. Wiping the sauce from his fingers with a napkin, he starts again up the street, more deliberately now, passing a gaunt figure hawking newspapers for a quarter. He buys one.

Paul's mouth burns from the strong taste of onions and, while it isn't yet one o'clock, he stops at a bar, orders a dark ale, and gingerly takes a first sip. It is good: it is exactly what he wants. He drinks the rest quickly and orders a second, flipping the pages of the newspaper but finding it difficult to concentrate. He sucks the head off the fresh glass of black beer; already the alcohol packs his brain like crushed ice. Light from the windows comes at him sharply, and the rhythm of drinking slows his thoughts, dials down the anxiety that lingers after the encounters with Bentham and Wolff. He drinks.

His thoughts tilt toward Claire. This is inevitable, he knows, even if she hadn't invited him up last night. He is constantly miserable over her, and so thinks about her constantly, and when he drinks he is miserable over and thinks about her even more. His hasn't been a distinguished reentry into bachelorhood. The sex with his ex-wife yesterday is the only sex he's had since the divorce. For a while he'd found himself in bars again; there were a couple of dates. But he no longer wants the difficult pleasure of surprise, the labor of uncertainty. Once upon a time it was exciting: a new person, new mind, new body. The narcissism of collecting the affections of different women. He has no need for that now. With Claire the work is done, and he is far enough along in life to realize that it *is* work, interrogating another person about her life and narrating your own for her; they are always stories you have told before, and, worse, hers are somehow ones you have already heard. Such is the cost of new romance. Even the disappointment of last night hasn't drained him of the wish to have her again. Paul doesn't believe it is nostalgia. Nostalgia is a fantasy, an ingrown wish. What he feels is a highly practical emotion, a desire to map the shortest possible route to contentment and peace. He isn't delusional, he hasn't any misconceptions about what a return to life with Claire would be like: it wouldn't come out gleaming or bright, like a freshly minted coin. But it would improve on what he has. If that's nostalgia, he thinks, so be it.

He drinks.

They met when she was twenty-four and he was thirty. She was working at a gallery in Chelsea and Paul, still balancing himself within the world, testing himself against it, was gathering his first real plumes of success as a writer. His name appeared frequently in those days, and in more places; editors kept his details to hand. He was dating casually, seeing a couple of women at a time, success like a renewable resource, a currency he could convert from work to sex and back again, its value always multiplying, and when he walked down the street in the middle of the day his blood beat with possibility. He ran regularly, used the gym. He felt young, strong, tight as a fist. He was a little thinner then.

Art was a serious interest long before he met her – even if his was an amateur's taste – and he'd decided to spend that particular afternoon at a few galleries, saving for last a group of new works by Gerhard Richter. This was the summer of 2000. Claire was standing at the desk, dealing with some papers, and Paul happened to catch her at a moment of private amusement. She was reading a document, and a dimple emerged at only one side of her mouth – an incidental gesture, meant for no one, yet it illuminated an intelligence and equanimity, a rich interior. The self she stored away from the world at hand. It didn't hurt that she had a lovely face, her brown hair pulled casually together into a clip, and, under a black skirt, a striking body, the kind that makes a man helplessly clench his teeth. Paul, standing at one of the paintings with his back to her, was working out what he might say, when to his great surprise she approached him.

'Are you looking to buy or just to rent?'

He was accustomed to being the clever one and, charmed, smiled a little more than he meant to.

'Is it that obvious?'

'Is what obvious? That you aren't here to throw around your millions?'

'You never know.'

'All but one or two of these were sold privately before we ever put them up. If you were the kind of man with the money to buy a Richter, your art consultant would have told you that.'

'What's the point of showing them at all? If you are so certain I don't have the cash to lay out for one.'

'Naturally, we have to maintain our considerable public profile.'

She smiled. He was not surprised to see that she had a wonderful smile.

'Then you're saying this one isn't up for sale.'

'I'm afraid not. You didn't have your heart set on it, I hope.'

'Where's it headed?'

'Dubai.'

By the time he left the gallery they'd arranged to have dinner. Over the next few weeks they met with growing urgency, confidence, heat; Paul stopped calling the other women. They secluded themselves. In his own life, at least, he knew of no precedent for the ease with which they discarded the previous versions of themselves in favor of a new, shared idea.

And for a while it remained so. Love fell on them as certainly and powerfully as sleep. He met her parents – they were polite and distant – and gave an account of his own. In the absence of a test, an episode of hardship, love was simple. Sex was regular and exhausting. He wanted to be depleted each night in her arms, to be fully spent, only so that she could replenish him. When they could, they made love in the afternoons. Winter came. In the cold their love condensed, hardened, like a seam of coal. Ice lashed the windowpanes. The wind screamed. They didn't care, they were in bed.

Spring. A thaw. Flowers budded, released their fists. Then an accident – Claire was late. For two days they talked it over. Marriage was mentioned and forgotten. Careers. Timing. And children, Claire said, made her wary. When she was a child she had felt like an interloper in her own parents' marriage; she wanted to be a better mother than that. I'm so young, she said. Paul may have replied, I'm not. He let it go, waited for her outside the doctor's.

That could have been it. With friends they were the same, but, alone together in a room, it was there, the little ghost. It isn't the most important thing in the world, she told him. We can move on. She wasn't being honest, but the lie helped. Slowly the oxygen returned to their relationship. The following summer was dreamy, uneventful, and, even if some of the burning of those early months had been lost, it was replaced by a new security and comfort. They were always generous, gracious, deferential. The leaves became dry, the air smelled like copper.

Six months after the planes hit the towers, they were married. Recalling the day, Paul drinks; he bites off a mouthful of beer as if it must be torn apart from the rest. More of her friends than his came to the wedding – she was younger and hadn't yet shed the relationships of college. By then his career as a writer was beginning to idle; he wasn't sure how it happened, what derailed him. He is even less certain now. The child they didn't have was never discussed, nor were the children they might one day have. It was assumed, or Paul assumed, that eventually, when the time felt right and the circumstances of their lives were suited to it, a luxury of forethought unknown for almost the entire span of human history, they would decide to conceive.

The fights started in the second year. Small things, at first. At some point Paul said what he was really thinking. So did she. Timing. Careers — hers by then describing a much more auspicious ascent. And she was still wary of children. He told her that he always imagined it as a son; at this she cried. He now remembers those arguments with bitter clarity, when in fact they were the exception. For the most part he and Claire were happy. They talked, fucked, traveled. It was what he wanted from a woman and from life. Even when they argued it was good, the reconciliation, the sturdiness and certainty of it, the knowledge that they always had safe terrain to return to. Children could wait.

With one swallow Paul halves the beer in his glass. There's a television above the bar and, sick of his thoughts, he asks to have it turned on. The screen jitters to life and the bartender looks at Paul, who nods. It's CNN. In silence a camera sweeps across a large crowd: yet another demonstration. He can feel the beer between his throat and his stomach. Dozens of faces fill the screen. A flag in the background — Syria's, Iran's, whatever — beats the air.

Paul calls back the bartender and orders another. When it arrives, he takes a greedy, immediate swallow. He's a little drunk. He barricades himself against further thoughts of Claire and looks again at the television. The camera pans toward the epicenter of the protest, and without the newscaster's voice there is no telling what may come next. It wouldn't surprise him if when the camera finally comes to a stop its gaze has settled on a dead body. He drinks.

Flames fill the screen, crisp and orange at the edges and at the center a deep, nightmarish black. It isn't yet apparent what's burning. Then the camera retreats and Paul can see the white cross and red field of the Danish flag. The camera leisurely absorbs the sight as the fire eats away the fabric's resistance. Nobody's dead. The image vanishes and into its place pops the anchorwoman's head. Eerie in her silence, strangely captive, she moves her mouth like a doll without its ventriloquist. Her well-trained face betrays no emotion.

Paul doesn't feel well. He takes another drink of his beer and immediately regrets it, as his body seems to be in mild revolt — nausea, headache, and feverishness set upon him at once. His ribs ache. For a moment the awful gurge of vomit seems to be rising within him, but he swallows dryly, pays for his drinks, and steps into the street. Once there he stands quite still and fixes his mind penitently on the simple acts of breathing and staring, as he contains and then patiently works down the sense of discomfort. The effort is made greater by the difference of sunlight — harsh, white, Martian — on slightly drunk eyes. The people who pass have their heads down, their bodies sheathed. Litter on the concrete swirls in the wind. He can walk: he begins to move. He refuses to admit that it might have been a mistake not to seek medical attention immediately after the attack last night — it was easier just to tough it out. Nothing was broken; bruises heal. Going to the hospital seemed unnecessary, to say nothing of the cost for an uninsured man. Nor does he intend to file a police report, which wouldn't do much good: he'd be able to offer only a cursory description, and the intended victim, anyway, was the boy; Paul was a byproduct. Better just to forget it.

Lightheaded, he descends at the nearest subway entrance and boards the L train bound for Manhattan; he disembarks at Union Square. The station's noise and its hot, oppressive air are immediate, as is the pollution of garbage: greasy paper and darkening fruit skins and milk-lined disposable cups that scamper along the tracks and fill the fortresslike black trash cans. Paul catches the sharp, vinegary smell of urine.

Departing and arriving trains keen and howl in their separate chambers. Drums beat the air. He ascends toward the street. Why is he so tired? He didn't have that much to drink. Policemen at one of the gates inspect bags. They are laughing, the officers, with a man whose belongings they have just searched. Up in the world again, Paul walks carelessly away, quickly, he thinks, although his footsteps seem also to be dribbling along the sidewalk; Claire used to say that he walks too fast. Even as he's moving, he feels sleep relax his brain, and when he reaches the address he wants, he sits heavily on the steps. In the warmth of his exhaustion the cold loses its strength, and his eyes, as heavy as garage doors, close.

At intervals he opens them, only partway, the world flicking in and out, and once a man, or a man's legs – Paul's eyes are aimed downward – are standing in front of him, as if waiting to have a conversation. Paul is too tired for that. He shuts his eyes again. The man is still there when he opens them, but the next time he is gone. Perhaps Paul imagined it, or dreamt it. He finally wakes to the sound of a voice. Standing above him are two people. One is Claire, the other a man he doesn't recognize. The one who was standing there a moment ago? Paul has no idea how long he's been here; his mouth, eyes, and brain are all webbed from sleep. He wishes he could have a glass of water, then registers the man's uniform: a police officer, his features screwed into a mixture of curiosity and disgust.

'You know him, ma'am?'

Claire nods, and, when the officer lingers, makes a gesture to indicate that he can go: Paul doesn't pose a threat. Even then, the policeman doesn't leave, but stands at a certain distance, his small face constricted, trying to fit Paul into one of the known categories of lawbreaker.

'Were you mugged?' asks Claire.

'No,' Paul says, only then realizing that she's looking at

the injury on his neck. 'It's nothing. I'm sorry. I don't know why I came here. I just felt so – tired.'

'You were tired? No one gets tired and falls asleep outdoors in the middle of winter. Tell me what happened.'

'Nothing happened. I'm sorry, it was stupid to have come here.' She doesn't contradict him. He makes an effort to rise to his feet, but stumbles. Claire steps forward. 'I'm fine,' he says.

'You aren't fine. What happened to your neck?'

'Nothing,' he says. 'I fell on some ice.'

'You've been drinking.'

She smells it on his breath. She also knows that for months immediately following the divorce he drank heavily. He often called late at night, his blood up, and come morning would forget what he'd said. She always refused to tell him, and eventually stopped answering the phone altogether. The policeman begins to walk away. Once he's out of hearing range Paul almost tells her everything: the boy, the thugs attacking him, his luck with the shard of glass. Wouldn't that impress her? He hasn't thought of it in terms of bravery until now, but certainly that's what it was. He put himself in harm's way to protect a stranger – his heart turns rubbery just from the memory. But something holds him back. Claire is hardly in the right frame of mind to hear it. The urge to speak dwindles, and the story begins to seem far off, irrelevant.

'If you're here to talk about last night—'

'I'm not. I'll go. I was just feeling out of sorts. It was – there was this meeting today, with an editor. He wants me to write a book about my father.'

'Ah.'

'I told him to forget about it.'

'Did he offer you money?'

'Basically. Yes, a lot of it.'

'Paul. You didn't consider it?'

'Don't make it sound like a choice I'll regret.'

Her face abruptly closes. 'Write the book or don't,' she says. 'It's your life, not mine.'

He looks away. At the end of the street stands a man in a wool cap, not moving, who seems to be staring right at him. Paul returns the look until the man walks out of view, which he does with unnatural deliberateness. Maybe he moved his head in response to someone's call; it is impossible to say from this distance.

Claire's eyes follow his down the street, to where the man was just standing, and she asks, the irritation still in her voice, what Paul is looking at.

'Nothing,' he says. 'For a minute I thought it was someone I know.'

From the day last May that she took the job at the museum Claire Brennan hasn't felt quite herself. Previously she slummed in galleries, advising the wealthy on purchases of art they didn't understand and enjoyed predominantly as a badge of status, and worked as a junior curator in smaller museums devoted to a single theme or region. Now, juggled by the little accidents of the New York art world, and having cashed in a decade's worth of connections, Claire has earned herself a position as a curator of painting and sculpture at the city's principal house of modern art. She's worked so hard to arrive at such success. Even so, the experience has been a strange one. Routine decisions suddenly have the pitch of high intrigue, subject to painstaking analysis and second-guessing. Reporters appear at her office. Little more than a year ago a wealthy donor willed to the museum an enormous sum of money, leaving its endowment swollen and its board of directors gluttonous, eager to make an earth-rattling acquisition. They set their sights on a canvas by a major postwar artist that had recently come onto the market, and the discussions of how much the museum was prepared to spend made Claire's face a little hot, the feeling of a child eavesdropping on adults as they discuss adult things. In the end it cost thirty million dollars.

This morning she had considerable difficulty rising. She called to tell her assistant that she wouldn't be in until the afternoon – she felt sick, she said, which was as good as true – and around one o'clock she was finally leaving when she found Paul on her doorstep. That didn't help. He was drunk, or at least on the way. How much of that was her fault? Last night troubles her because she doesn't know why she did what she did. He ambushed her, appeared at her door, but she didn't have to allow his obvious emotional need to overwhelm her. For whom was she feeling sorry when she invited him up? Her decision had the impetuous reck- lessness of sex during college, when it mattered to have sex but mattered less whom you had it with, when its very casualness gave a little thrill to the ego. Might she simply have wanted proof that she could still have him? She isn't lonely. She wouldn't have gone out of her way to seduce her ex-husband. She was careful, from the moment their clothes came off, not to kiss him on the mouth.

Now she moves briskly through the museum's lower galleries, half filled with the sluggish weekday crowds, mostly tourists, who drift from painting to painting with the indolence of mosquitoes. Invariably, they collect in front of the pieces everyone knows. They stare because they know they are supposed to. Few of the tourists have any interest in what currently hangs on the west wall of the atrium, a sequence of four linked, abstract paintings by Cy Twombly. Each depicts one of the seasons, and her favorite, since seeing them for the first time years ago in London, has always been *Inverno* – winter – in which a giant black sun seems to sink through the bottom of the frame. She could use a moment with these paintings to take her mind off Paul, but there isn't time now, and, in any case, standing in the presence of a painting should really be a private act. Claire's professional life, of course, demands that she spend much of her day looking at art in the company of others, but she has worked diligently to preserve a separate province within herself.

In her office the soft, pungent odor of fresh print fills the air. Her assistant has left a new round of reports on her desk. They detail a roster of paintings up for sale and the slate of artists who will soon have new groups of works the museum may like. It's a busy season. Miami was disappointing this year, but in the coming months a number of interesting young artists will hold solo exhibitions around the city. March brings the Armory show. So much to keep an eye on. That's why she's here: to discover innovation and uproot its best examples, to evangelize for the art she believes in. And if she does her job well, the museum can avoid paying an outrageous sum forty years from now for a painting they could have had cheap. Such is the case with the recent purchase, made available to the museum when its artist was a younger man, not yet a commodity; the offer was declined. She tries not to consider the money as a material weight: rows of houses, bushels of grain, crates of medicine. At the end of the week the painting will hang here. But how can anyone look at it without thinking of the money? Who at this point can truly see it?

There's a knock on the door. Splits open in the seams of her reverie. Sitting, she takes some documents and scatters them on the desk, then calls, 'Come in.'

The man who enters is David Kim. Under his arm is a fat stack of papers. He's always busy with something, a restless engine of efficiency. It's hard to imagine him daydreaming.

'I've got the final plans for the April show,' he says, running a thumb along the edge of her desk.

David's supreme sense of confidence both unsettles and impresses her. He's the head curator of the architecture department and, as far as she can tell, doesn't doubt the decisions he makes, not beforehand and certainly not afterward. His parents were both diplomats – Korean father, Canadian mother – and, as he explained to her once, his childhood was accordingly disjointed. Rather than damage him, it was a gift: spending his early years in several countries seems to have made him at home wherever he is, whomever he's with.

'You can drop it there.' She indicates one of the few spaces on her desk.

'You're busy?' He shifts his weight, and for a moment she feels mischievously proud: she has made David Kim unsure of himself.

'No, not at all. I just got in – no meetings this morning. I was a little lost in thought.'

He smiles and puts the papers on her desk, gently squaring the edges, and turns to leave.

'David, wait. You don't have to go.'

He stops, smiling. 'That's a relief. You can save me from another round of calls to donors.'

'You do all right. Bernard won't stop talking about how much you squeezed out of them last month.'

He dips his head: a man aware of his own charm. When he looks up, he says: 'I almost forgot to tell you. My sister had the baby.' When she doesn't speak, he adds, 'It's a little strange when you don't have any kids yourself. Nice, too. Being an uncle, I mean.'

Claire's eyes go briefly out of focus. 'Congratulations.'

'And congratulations to you, too.'

'What for?'

'Doesn't it go up this week?'

'That's what they tell me.'

'It's going to look wonderful there in the main hall, with the Newman.'

'You'll have to see for yourself,' she says. 'Friday. One of Bernard's wine-and-cheese affairs.'

'If he isn't careful he's going to drink us right out of an endowment. Someone ought to remind him how much good champagne costs.'

David hovers between desk and door, managing to seem much closer than he is. Since setting down the papers he's hardly moved. Claire has the urge to rise, maybe go to him — she doesn't know what she would do next. It feels so formal, sitting here behind a desk while he stands. He could have taken the other chair. But their conversation has begun to dry up; it would be strange now to ask him to sit. Then again, perhaps it's for the best — they're at work. David gives no sign that he feels any of the same discomfort. He says: 'I'll get out of your hair.'

'You're not in my hair.' He's done at least one thing right: she's stopped thinking about Paul.

Opening the door, he turns. 'I hope we're still on for tomorrow night.'

Claire nods. She smiles.

The sun is low and the alcohol has worn off completely by the time the train puts him back in Brooklyn. Ordinary thoughts fill his mind; mundanity returns. Paul thinks of an article whose deadline is approaching and, preferring this idle mental drift to the expectant screen of his computer, takes his time; he walks with luxurious slowness and turns into Prospect Park to use the paths there. It was late spring when he moved into the neighborhood, and, in a state of torpor and absentminded grief following the divorce, he convinced himself that it was the best place to be — near the park, which during the hot months was ripe with life. It would make depression impossible. He spent hours in the park by himself: fireworks on Independence Day, concerts at the band shell, even a few short jogs on the circuit road, although he quickly gave those up; fitness wasn't a priority. The air was grassily bright and smelled sweetly of tanning lotion; it shivered around the charcoal pits of barbecues and fluttered with the screams of happy children. Kites turned in the sky, twitches of color. The lawns were wide, undulating, and green. They would endure a cycle of freezing and brief thaws after the grass died, and the ground would soften into a greasy, gelatinous mud. Dogs shit everywhere.

But Paul lost interest in the park long before the cold came, even before autumn brought an occasional eerie current of fog. By then he had found the bars on Fifth Avenue, down the hill in Park Slope; there seemed to be dozens. Many were popular with the crops of fresh arrivals to Brooklyn, kids from the suburbs of Cleveland and Baltimore and St Louis and Omaha, and from even smaller and more far-flung cities no one ever thinks of. Radiating a strange panic, they came in droves, like an exodus in reverse. They came with expensive educations and bank accounts full of their parents' money, and when the air was warm they filled the gardens of those bars, drinking two-dollar cans of tasteless beer. The men had new beards. Paul eavesdropped on their conversations, which were unfailingly dull, each one a version of another he'd heard. Everyone had a favorite bar in Brooklyn, it seemed, and it was never the bar he was drinking at. Most of the time Paul avoided the gardens altogether: he preferred to drink indoors, in the brutal scullery-like darkness, on a hard stool with his knees pinned against the oak and bottles arrayed before him in twinkling rows, even as the reproachful squares of sunlight near the exit gazed at him. He did crossword puzzles and read magazines. If the Mets were playing an afternoon game, he watched that. He didn't have friends, at least not ones he cared enough to call, and his work was finished by two o'clock; he could drink all afternoon, and as late into the night as he wanted.

It's a much different Brooklyn from his father's, not that Frank watched the transformations of the past decade with great interest or concern. His apartment in Greenpoint, where he has lived since the death of Paul's mother, sits on a block of India Street that, before the kids began arriving in hordes, was home only to the elderly and to families, mostly Polish, who had emigrated to America before and after the war. Crime wasn't an issue. But the neighbors still had their concerns – tree-planting, clean sidewalks, broken streetlights – and they sometimes sent around a petition to have one problem or another dealt with by the city. This was the early eighties, Ed Koch was the mayor, and nothing ever changed. Paul seldom saw his father interact with anyone but himself, and so it was always mildly amusing to see an outsider, usually a small woman with a rippling, ugly dress, attempting to interest him in some minor fiasco.

Frank didn't have friends, but there were men he saw regularly, at a restaurant on Manhattan Avenue, where he would order a coffee and a plate of fried meat pierogis or schnitzel. He sat alone – or rather, with Paul, before Paul was old enough plausibly to look after himself. He wasn't there to converse, but when you make a point of haunting the same restaurant with military regularity – in Frank's case, around six o'clock on most weekday evenings, and during the afternoons on both Saturday and Sunday – the other regulars eventually take a certain comfort in your presence. He wore a hat and trench coat, which he did no matter where he went and in all but the hottest weather, and would hang these on the pegs by the door. People usually asked about Paul, especially the waitresses, who all spoke heavily accented English. They assumed that Frank and Paul were grandfather and grandson, and they were unfailingly touched by the sight of such devotion across three generations. Frank never quite corrected them; this was when he was around seventy, and no one would have mistaken him for a younger man.

With these men Frank had conversations about things that otherwise didn't seem to interest him – the election, baseball, movies, subway repairs, international politics, the Pope. Their talk was rigidly male, terse and disjointed and topical, and no one ever spoke of women, except in the most abstract terms. Now and then one of the men warned Paul against marriage. Shaking his own left hand like a prosthetic limb, he would cry, 'It's a life in prison!' At this the others chuckled, croaked, and wheezed; they all smoked heavily. No one asked Frank about his own naked ring finger. They spoke in crosscurrents: it was impossible to follow the flow of the conversation, with its irregular interruptions of laughter and its sudden reversals, because there wasn't a flow to the conversation: they were men, strangers, filling silence. It was nonetheless an arena of participation, and Frank, as nowhere else in life, participated. Frank, who didn't go to the cinema, expressed an opinion on De Niro's performance in *Raging Bull*. Frank, who didn't follow any team, concurred with another man's estimation of Reggie Jackson's chances of winning the MVP. Where did he get his information? Later in life, himself now an adult male, Paul understood how his father, who read nothing but newspapers, was able to stand his ground in a conversation on almost any topic.

The greater surprise was that Frank bothered at all. Elsewhere he was spectral in his absence from the texture of everyday life, but in that restaurant, among its other regulars, he became a living thing, with blood and lungs and a mind, and Paul could see the flickering outline of the man who once was. He wasn't animated, and he never got especially heated in his opinions — because, of course, he didn't really care, his interests, whatever they were, weren't baseball or politics — but he looked other men in the eye, he listened, he was obviously content to be there. He would stay long after his plate had been cleared and his coffee had grown cold.

It was the sort of place you find anywhere in Brooklyn or Queens: the emigrant salon. In Brighton Beach it's the Russians, in Astoria it's the Greeks. In Jackson Heights the Indians, Williamsburg the Dominicans and the Italians, Midwood the Pakistanis. The men at the restaurant in Greenpoint were Polish, and Frank was born to Germans, but Frank was never excluded, or never seemed to be. Not all the men were his age. Many were only in their forties. They were immigrants, jobless, overweight, in debt, often unmarried, and they cloistered themselves in a shoddily appointed restaurant whose chunky walls bulged with panels of ancient, blood-dark mahogany and whose light was a jaundiced chintzy yellow. They sat all day. It was the kind of restaurant one passes without entering. The tablecloths were made of slick heavy polyester, as were the napkins, which meant that they were almost impossible to use. Paul hated it there. But as he began his own inevitable filial drift, at fourteen, fifteen, sixteen, and was no longer bound to accompany his father, he found himself surprised by another filial inevitability — guilt. It wasn't that he felt nostalgia for the restaurant, yet he could think of no better term for what fell upon him when, at college in Boston, he would overhear a snatch of talk from the tables of old men who played chess all day at one of the outdoor cafes.

In the last years before Paul left for college, Frank gradually stopped going to his restaurant. He bought groceries – an even sadder thing to contemplate, Frank in his hat and coat, toting a shopping basket up and down the fluorescent aisles – and began eating at home. He never explained this change of routine.

Patches of ground are still hoary from yesterday's snowfall. Paul turns in the direction of the exit. Late-afternoon light fills the bushes near the stone gate and their gray branches burn and glisten with individual intricacy. He steps from the quiet of the park into the quiet of the avenue. A car rolls by, and then another, but, at an hour before people have begun to return from work, there is no one. Innocent, pastoral silence flows down the street. The signs of life are distant: the drone of the nearest expressway; the chthonic moaning of trains rising from the grates. In the present silence Paul hears again the jagged explosion of the bottle against the ground. His fingers flex around an imagined shard of glass. He looks at the fading cuts on his hand, and recalls with shock that less than a day has gone by.

Like the rest, his own street is deserted. His footsteps slow almost to a halt. No one is there, but no one was supposed to be there last night, either. He recalls the primitive enthusiasm of the two men for their task, especially that of the one called Terence, and their patient enjoyment of it, the recreational tempo. Now his street is back to normal – he is relieved to find that no one is on his block – but it has been made strange, and the silence, which might usually be a comfort, a confirmation that nothing is happening, instead feels like an ominous preamble. Even reaching for his keys reminds him of last night's events.

He notices it when he is still a few doors away, although

at first it could be anything, its shape and color indistinct. It is just a thing. He is now one building away. The thing is short and dark and certainly was not there when Paul left the apartment this morning. Only at the foot of the stairs can he be sure that it is the squat round bottom half of a glass bottle – its splintered peaks filled with an oddly soft, buttery light – and that its top half lies around in a sparkling ring of bits and pieces.

3

The price of gas has an effect — too great an effect — on Ben Wald's sense of well-being. In the past week natural gas has fallen eighteen points and as a result the spread has collapsed. When the market moves against him Ben feels inadequate as a man. Those eighteen points are a lack, a physical deterioration. A pound of flesh carved right out of his side. And yet this does not translate into real despair. Not quite that. He hasn't become so myopic that he forgets entirely what really matters: his wife and son. Men exist who do, of course — some are good friends of his. They cut off their families, abandon themselves in the work; they perceive the world as a tangle of ascending and descending lines on a chart, peaks and valleys of luminous significance. They simply lose sight. Of? Of life. Of the miracles with which God has stocked the planet: the pleasures of the natural world, of family, of music and art. Not Ben. He swore long ago, when he was still a young trader and witnessed the ease with which the inner lives of others caved in, never to become like that. Beth and Jake are the foundation of his happiness; the money he earns belongs to them. His present trouble with the government, if nothing else, has reminded him of this — they're threatening to take it all away. Tomorrow begins a premature penance, when, to pull heat off the company and to avoid becoming a distraction, Ben will step down for an indefinite leave of absence. It's a precaution. Already he dreads the aimlessness of days without purpose, a mere counting of hours, no task at hand, no chance for quantifiable gain. There's still a good chance, or so his lawyer tells him, of emerging unscathed. He can't think about the consequences if he doesn't. Prison has been mentioned. What he's accused of doing, which involves a sequence of transactions in a certain futures market, is no different from what men in his position do every day. If it goes away he will count it as a blessing, a test. He'll be a stronger man, a man more devoted to the people he loves, the values he cherishes. But even then he won't be able salve the ache that comes when the numbers don't cooperate; the suffering is built into him. Not even the touch of his wife's hand eases it. That it cannot is what pains him the most.

It is Monday afternoon: the markets are winding down. He waits for the end of the day in his office. A few people have stopped in to say goodbye, but most avoid him, and he understands. The younger analysts don't know how to talk to him, and don't know how he will respond; he has in recent weeks become a difficult thing. He glances once more at the latest article. Slipped into the scrutiny of his supposed crime, nothing more than a handful of business decisions — *For God's sake!* he thinks, umbrage coiling in his throat — they have printed it: the identity of his father, what his father did. Of everything they have come after him with, this is the most unpardonable, as shameful and disproportionate as a stoning. Those were Frank's choices, not Ben's; the only relevant choice Ben made in that regard was to reject the man. While he bristles at what they want to make of him, a symbol of the gluttony and venality of the new Gilded Age, at least he understands it — the public has a thirst for this, it caws to see wealthy men deplumed. But to affix the name Metzger to him is a more odious punishment, a tarring he doesn't deserve. He's embarrassed. It is his fault. He drew this cloud upon himself and – far, far worse – upon his family. He instructed Jake not to read the papers, but who can guess what a friend will tell him? Ben knows that he, too, should stop reading about it, and just throw out the paper, but something halts him: his eye is drawn again and again to the words there, the conspicuous inky ugliness of them: 'Ben Metzger.'

But he's not that. He's Wald. Wald began life at seventeen, on the day he told Frank Metzger that he was done with him, the family, the name, everything. Wald went into the world, graduated from college, discovered a talent for numbers and predictions, earned all he has, *made* all he has. Self-made. Ben loves the phrase, the mental warmth it gives him, all that it suggests. The best men are those who invent themselves: who fit the world around them, tailor it like a suit.

A figure hovers at the door. The knock comes, and Kevin, one of the young analysts, flies in on his heels, bursting with the exasperation and heat of something gone wrong. Ben's been expecting this. Late trading has lit an emergency among the analysts; the newest rumors are dark currents radiating from Russia, China, Brazil. But until now the noise has registered only distantly, as if from miles beyond the front. He understands why: his legal troubles have given him an aura of fragility, no one knows quite what to do with him, and so they are all treating him with special caution. At the end of today he leaves. It makes him feel old and irrelevant, a lost cause. Persona non grata is not too strong a term.

'Natural gas again,' Kevin reports. 'We're getting pounded out there.'

The agitation of his hands makes it apparent how hard

his heart is running: he looks as if he's just walked away from a car accident. Kevin graduated less than a year ago. The money's shaking inside him. Ben remembers that feeling, the juice of adrenaline everywhere in you at once, and seeing it in this young man makes him feel suddenly apart from whatever's happening, free of it. As much as he's been waiting for this — for something to do — he now locks up with reluctance.

'Go talk to Grant.' Grant runs the energy desk. When Ben started the hedge fund, Grant, who came up with him at Goldman Sachs, was the first man he hired. Tomorrow he'll be in charge. He's stood by Ben even as the trouble with the S.E.C. has gone from threat to reality, as many of his other friends have stopped calling. Kevin leaves, shutting the door behind him, but Ben remains alert, as if someone's still in the room, an unfamiliar anxiety buzzing below his thoughts. He's accustomed to a low boil of anger at work — it keeps him hungry. To make as much as he does requires him to think of his job as a zero-sum game: he wants to take money from the next guy, dig in his pockets for loose change. A little competitive burning is good, a touch of brutality. But today there's a parallel poison in the blood, this one distracting rather than concentrating the mind. It has nothing whatsoever to do with the job or the government's investigation. It's been there all day, yet only now can he name its source: his brother.

Paul's appearance yesterday magnified tenfold the bullshit the newspapers are printing. Ben still can't identify what softness made him agree to it. When he was still in his thirties and Paul was no more than a child, he'd see his brother from time to time — always on the condition that Frank wasn't present, and in part because his mother encouraged it, although it was never clear to him why — but already the relationship was spoiled. Theirs would never be the normal experience of brotherhood. As Paul aged it became even more difficult to look at him and see anything other than an appendage of Frank's. He had no real sense of who their father was, of what he had done — he still doesn't. From the start Ben couldn't tolerate the insult of his younger sibling's innocence.

In the years since, he's been able to consider Paul, when he considers him at all, from a comfortable remove; he has grown to feel mere indifference toward him. Casually, he's kept up with the events of his brother's life — graduation, marriage, a string of professional successes, although that seems to have tapered off, and now the divorce — but does so as if reading the news from another country. For the past three years he hasn't seen him at all. The interval was, for Ben, a product of fatigue. He and his brother have had so many arguments, almost always about their father, and they occur at instances of practical need since Ben has remained, legally, a part of the story. Frank's death is set to become one more such occasion.

Money, Ben knows, is the one universal language. Money is a declaration. When you speak aloud you can retract it, claim a Freudian slip, an errant tongue, but money never misspeaks. Politicians know it, journalists know it, lawyers know it. Frank knew that when he put his in a suitcase and took it to Germany.

And that money, Frank's inheritance, ought to have gone toward raising a family — had he used it wisely Ben's childhood might have been less difficult, his mother might have been happier, had new clothes, a firmer sense of her place in the world. She might not have left Frank. Ben could have known what it was like to have a family, a real one, a warm house, Sunday dinners. All the things he makes sure to provide Jake and Beth, and which the government now wants to strip him of. Frank spent his family's money to kill Jews.

Now, as he dies, Frank will give back to the world a modest sum which – Ben supposes, though he hasn't done the calculations – is comparable to what three thousand dollars was worth in 1937. Paul wants it. What he doesn't understand is that it isn't about him; Ben has no interest in punishing him. It means nothing to him what money his brother does or does not have. Except this money. This money, this blood money, cannot stay in Metzger hands. Ben hasn't decided exactly what he plans to do with it – donate it to the Anti-Defamation League or the American Israel Public Affairs Committee, he guesses, use it to turn back the second-rate Hitlers who govern Iran and Syria, who dream of a second Holocaust, a nuclear winter over Tel Aviv. He could even pack the cash into a briefcase and hand-deliver it, in homage.

His wife, who hasn't been trained to abhor compromise, has told him he's being unfair – that he should at least consent to split the will down the middle with his brother. Ben long ago silenced the part of himself that might have agreed with her. Inner doubt constitutes a dangerous weakness, a malfunction in need of repair. He isn't being unreasonable. Unreasonable was their father – he got out beyond unreasonable, at the far edge of moral sickness, as an accomplice to the most advanced case of evil the world has ever known. That man owes more than is possible to give, but his repentance must begin with the sacrifice of all he owns; at the end of such a life he must be stripped of everything. Of this Ben is certain; nothing can dislodge this belief. The sentiment manifests itself as a physical conviction – in the back of his jaw, between his teeth. An article of purest faith.

* * *

Self-delusion is a process marked by tiny, inner steps of gradual logic, like inching under a blanket. Paul returned to the apartment more than two hours ago and since then night has fallen, but he hasn't reacted to what he found at his doorstep. He has done little but sit in a cushiony slump on the sofa, and hasn't given much thought to Terence, although certainly it was he who smashed that bottle on the step. Of course, Paul ought to be thinking about Terence, and about the intelligent next move, but in his fear, or apprehension — he is not sure which it is, which expresses the appropriate degree of severity — he misplaces his concerns. Claire has been a constant thought. She at least offers him the retreat of self-pity. With no obvious change in temperature, he finds himself sweating and deeply thirsty. He feels a headache bunching up behind his eyes. He stands abruptly.

At the kitchen sink he opens the tap and swallows glass after glass of whitish lukewarm water. He can drink no more. The tap, still running full-blast, is the only noise in the apartment, and like many domestic sounds in an empty home it comes with a contradictory set of connotations: comfort, anxiety, loneliness. He feels a little better.

It is high time, in any case, to call the police. There's probably little they can do, but a report at least ought to be filed. The buttons of the phone respond to his fingers with a satisfying rubbery tension, and the feeling that fills him is a reassuring one, a sense of resolve that has gone missing lately.

He has called the emergency line, and a woman summarily transfers him to the local precinct, where another officer, a man with a young-sounding voice, answers. He speaks in a tone bleached with indifference. It is late. Paul says, 'I want to report a crime.'

'What is the nature of the crime?'

'A man left a broken bottle at the door of my building – a threat.'

'A bottle? You saw him break it? He say anything?'

'No, he was gone.'

'What is your name, sir?'

Paul tells him.

'Can you explain why you're so sure a bottle on your doorstep is a threat?'

'This man, he – actually, he and his friend – they were beating up this kid. I stopped them. This was last night. They got me pretty bad too.'

'What is the victim's name?'

'I don't know. I think he was Arab. Muslim.'

'Where was this?'

Paul gives the name of his street.

'Hold on.' The man is gone; Paul hears the snickering of computer keys. 'Sir, we have no report of an assault in that area in the past two weeks.'

'Maybe the kid didn't report it.'

'Why didn't you report it, sir?'

'I don't know. I'm reporting it now. But this bottle – this threat.'

'Sir, this is New York. We got a lot of broken bottles lying around.'

'But it wasn't just lying around. It was standing upright. Somebody *placed* it there, very consciously, like a little monument of broken glass. He meant for me to find it.'

'A monument?'

Exhaustion and irritation pump through him. He sighs. 'Like a monument, yes.' As the man said, this is New York. They must get many callers with unserious claims. This man is accustomed to interpreting things in their most ordinary and innocuous light.

'Is this man – is he there right now?'

'No.'

'I'm sorry, sir, but it doesn't sound like there's much we can do, except maybe give him a fine for littering. If it is a threat, it's a pretty weird one. If you want to bring it down to the station, the bottle or whatever, and fill out the necessary paperwork—'

'It seems like he might come back.'

'Sir, if you're in immediate danger you should call nine-one-one.'

Only after Paul collapses into a chair does he recall the figure at the end of Claire's street, who by now he is certain was Terence, and he wishes he had mentioned that. But he's too tired to call again, and he doubts it would change much, anyway; perhaps the man with whom he spoke has the proper outlook. If Terence were serious, he would have done more than leave – indeed – a little monument of broken glass at his doorstep.

Fully awake now, and constructively energized by irritation, he goes to his office, intending to use the next few hours to work. Most urgent is the review of a political history of Islam. The deadline is next week. Of late Paul's habits of productivity have been desultory, almost to the point of vanishing: he finished reading the book ten days ago; the filaments of thought have grown cold, and if he doesn't return to it soon, he will lose the thing altogether. The subject interests him, but, in Paul's opinion, the author overlooks a fundamental aspect of faith, considering it as a symptom of culture and failing to see that the belief in God is a basic urge, like hunger or sex, and that like those things it sinks into the mind and touches all the other objects there – that it has the power, like superstition, to alchemize otherwise unremarkable moments, when because of an evolutionary misprint the human mind presses mystical importance from mundane coincidence. A given mind is either ready for these moments or it isn't. Paul's was, once. But the religion of his youth has receded so far into his past that it is difficult for him to resuscitate the heat of it, the ardor, that firm, unironic sincerity.

He has a limit of eight hundred words. After reading through his notes for fifteen minutes, Paul feels the crackle of a headache once more tuning up between his temples. He goes to the kitchen for a glass of water and swallows three aspirin. This time the headache doesn't go away. It has the character of divinely induced punishment. After a while it becomes so painful that he leaves his chair and paces the apartment, then returns and extinguishes all the lights. His mood improves somewhat. Still, he doesn't want to work on the review; he pulls out the draft of an unrelated magazine piece — light, on a book about cocktail recipes based on famous novels and films — and spends an hour tidying it up. When he puts it aside, he realizes how heavy his eyes feel and, shutting them, leans back in the chair.

Claire is the obvious subject for thought, and though she does occur to him — in a short, pornographic reel that leaves him feeling empty and unsavory — surprisingly it is his father who comes to mind. Recent months have allowed him to spot an inheritance from Frank that prior years, with their run of professional and personal success — which he now readily admits was luck as much as anything else — had obscured. It is a matter of temperament. He should be working, and he isn't. From Frank he got this penchant for idle mental occupancy and this comfort with drift, the use of one's mind as a deck chair rather than an engine. In his father it always appeared to be absentmindedness, mere procrastination, but this masked something else, Paul realized later: a belief that the brute calculus of the world — you work to live — did not apply to certain individuals, his father among them.

This tendency of Frank's was a shell of what it must once have been; for the duration of Paul's early childhood he put in his hours at the insurance company, and he retired with a pension. But when he came home with 'a little work to do,' Paul would invariably find him leaning back in his chair at the dinner table, chewing a pencil, staring glassily at some far corner of the ceiling, and, embarrassingly, not doing what he said he had to do.

Frank must once have had an entrepreneurial instinct. His actions as a young man were contemptible, but they did not lack for energy. This zeal survived in his later life, his life as Paul's father, only as an ember of sociability, one that flickered when he was at the restaurant, or during their walks through Greenpoint, when he adopted the ambient purpose-lessness of the flâneur. He just wanted to be out of the house. This instinct would die, too, as one by one Frank shut down his social outlets and shrunk his life to that of a man alone in a room.

Paul feels a fresh gust of frustration, one that indicts Ben, who constantly swells with the vanity of moral sentiment. There's no evidence that Frank fully appreciated what was happening in Germany, not in '37 and '38; few did. A man cannot be made to suffer the indignity of blame into the last chapter of his life for the acts of his youth, even the indefensible ones, even those for which naivety isn't an excuse. He doesn't believe that Frank should be forgiven, not in the strict sense of the word. For one thing, he never asked to be. Paul simply thinks that his father isn't, that no one is, a single, fossilized thing.

Feeling a soft, magnetic tug, he opens his eyes and pulls out a fresh sheet of paper. He uncaps a pen and presses two sentences onto the empty page: 'My father had it in him to strike me only once. I was thirteen.' He sits back in the chair and studies the words: already it feels a betrayal, not of his father, but of himself, of the version of himself who resisted Bentham, who said no. Yet before he can stop he falls again toward the paper and more pours out:

It was a small thing — five dollars I stole from his wallet to see a movie with some friends. They talked me into it, after I told them I didn't have the money to go. When I got home he drove a hand across my face. Before hitting me, he used the other hand to keep my head in place, cradling my chin in his palm, a gesture both gentle and practical, bluntly paternal. My lip was split. He assumed I knew the reason. I did, but I didn't understand his reaction; I'd done worse in the past, or at least it seemed I had.

Not until he was fifteen or sixteen did Paul ask any questions. He was upset that he hadn't seen his brother in several years and aware that this was somehow his father's fault. Frank sat there in his chair, where he almost always was; then he nodded to himself and, with a sputtering grunt, rose. 'Stay there.' When he returned he handed Paul a large envelope. It was full to bursting, and when he tried to open it the brittle metal fastener broke off in his hand. He pulled out a lump of crisp, delicate newsprint: He read one page after another before becoming self-conscious at reading about his father in front of him, and stole away to his room to finish. The articles were ordered chronologically, from the earliest days of the Long Island meetings right up until the end. He'd kept everything, even the stories about the trial. Paul returned to find his father sitting exactly where he had left him.

He said, 'That really was you?'

With visible effort Frank unglued his lips to speak; he

might have shaken his head, too, but the gesture was ambiguous. He opted for silence. He was seventy-five years old by then, and he had nothing else to say about the matter.

4

Tuesday. On his way to the hospital Paul passes a pharmacy.
Red and pink crêpe paper festoons the eaves and an arc of
cardboard hearts hangs in the window. Similar displays have
filled the city for weeks, but only today, the holiday itself,
does Paul become aware of the date. For a divorced man of
thirty-six Valentine's Day ceases to mean much. That's for
lovesick teenagers. Even in the wake of recent events, he's
too old to find in such scenery the stuff of sadness or self-
pity. By tomorrow it will have vanished. Easter takes its place,
the next page on the calendar that dictates the pace of
American life, the natural seasons replaced by forces
that apportion the year into blocks of commercial time,
occasions for spending.

A pair of orderlies stands at the main entrance,
slouched like scarecrows, sucking down cigarettes. They
don't wear jackets over their scrubs and shiver a little;
one turns out his mouth in a cursory smile. Ambulances
wait in a silent row for work to be called in. A slow
morning.

Nothing's changed in the familiar room. Machines beep
softly; drops of clear serum make the slow journey down a
tube into his father's blood. Above all, Paul is aware of the
emptiness, the austerity. Shouldn't a man be surrounded by
flowers and weeping relatives – the evidence that the world

will suffer in his absence? Not this man. His departure from this room will alter almost nothing about it. Paul has never thought to bring flowers; then again, his father wouldn't want him to. Frank has always been an unsentimental man, unconcerned with the decorative, the ephemeral.

Color has drained from the face, though it wasn't a face with much color in the first place. In the last decade Frank spent as much time as possible indoors, preferring that kind of loneliness to the loneliness of crowds, of walking among people who don't know you and don't care to. Not that Paul was keeping much track. His visits, always sparse, had become even more erratic, although the trip to his father's apartment was a matter of taking the F train to Bergen Street and then transferring to the G train. He packaged his father as a set of practical problems – dealing with the insurance company, managing a fixed income from dividends on his pension. It gave them something to talk about, and was easier than trying at that late hour to forge anything more complex.

After Paul's divorce it was even more difficult to visit his father, to witness the crushed, compacted state of his existence. He hardly moved, he never wrote or read. Paul once hunted through the apartment for a journal, a stack of letters, any evidence of an interior life, but came away empty-handed. His visits lasted for an hour or so, during which he and his father would sit together and watch television, whatever came on, and then Paul would leave, a little queasy. Without his wife he came to understand, in a way he hadn't before, that a person's life is comprised of and defined by the relationships he has – that a self-sustained existence, however worthy and pure that idea might once have sounded, is a fraudulent one. That sort of life is for monks and saints, not actual human beings.

During their last conversation, in the hospital before he

slipped into the coma, Frank said nothing of regret, of final wishes, of love or fear or loss. He only made sure that Paul had called the private nurse he'd hired and told her not to show up that week at the apartment.

And now, his father unconscious, Paul continues to come, a few days a week, because there isn't anyone else who will. It does not feel voluntary. It is the kind of thing one does because it is, as they say, a good idea.

A shape sweeps in and out of the room. The nurse. Perhaps she believes she's come at a bad moment. Paul stands to go, but, as he makes his first steps toward the door, a swell of nausea upends him. He tries to ignore it, he'll feel better once he's outside, away from this place. But he staggers and has to brace himself against a chair. The onrush of illness and lightheadedness brings a thick, ponderous sensation into his limbs, a headache brutalizing the middle regions of his brain, sudden thirst burning on his tongue like frost. He sits. The room seems almost to tilt. Control leaves him: he closes his eyes, unbuckles himself from consciousness, and lets his head fall lightly upon the foot of his father's bed.

Later, when the nurse wakes him, he asks how much time has gone by. She isn't sure. Outside, the afternoon light is fading, the sky the color of oyster shell; it has been perhaps half an hour. The nurse asks if he often goes to sleep like this in the middle of the day. Feeling unsteady, he answers that this isn't the first time it has happened recently. She asks if he has headaches; he nods. Can he walk? At this he stands and follows her out of the room.

Though the nausea and pain abate, Paul doesn't feel restored to health. He trails the nurse to a different room, where she leaves him; he doesn't know how long he waits before a doctor comes. Although he and Paul are about the same age, the doctor's tone and bearing immediately establish him as the elder: his questions are brisk, exact, professional. Eventually he asks Paul if he's hit his head in the last few days.

He nods. 'Sunday.'

'How did it happen?'

'A fall. On some ice.' Paul touches the fading mark on his neck. 'Right on the pavement.'

'Did you lose consciousness?'

'Maybe a little. Briefly.'

The doctor makes a note. 'Sounds like a concussion. It's not too serious, but these multiple episodes of fainting suggest post-concussion syndrome. You seem pretty lucid, so I'm not worried about bleeding. Aspirin will take care of the pain. The drowsiness should go away. If it doesn't, you need to call someone.'

Paul thanks him.

'You're still a little light on your feet. I'd feel better, Mr Metzger, if someone came to escort you home and get you into bed. Is there anyone?'

He thinks for a minute, then borrows a pen and dashes off a phone number. Handing it to the doctor, he says: 'Him.'

'I wasn't sure you'd come,' says Paul when they're free of the hospital. Ben makes no reply and merely nods in the direction of his car. He needn't; it is at once apparent which is his, the black Mercedes-Benz parked two blocks away, whose conspicuous expense and insistent glamour cruelly distinguish it from nearby vehicles. Ben seems not to register this aesthetic glitch. Instead, as they cross the street, he glances at Paul, as if trying to puzzle out on his own what happened. At the car he quickly unlocks the doors, slides in, and starts the engine. Paul supports himself against the passenger door and presses his forehead against the roof. The metal is punishingly cold and shoots straight through him, all the way down to his feet. He breathes deeply and hopes not to faint. Ben gets out.

'I'm just a little dizzy,' says Paul. 'Give me a minute.'

He anticipates an impatient reply from Ben, who must have left in the middle of work, but his brother says nothing. Around them everything is calm, benign, uninterested. Paul starts to feel better, more stable. He looks at his brother. Ben is dressed casually — Paul always pictures a suit — and leans against the door, both elbows resting on the roof: his arms reach across the car, hands half open. These hands, filled with such power, are normally implements of threat, coercion, resistance. At the moment they project a milder kind of strength, an offer of protection. But Paul is still lightheaded and unable to evaluate his brother's appearance; he gave the doctor his number almost in a spirit of self-deprecation.

'Do you need to go back in there?' Ben jerks his head toward the hospital.

'No,' says Paul as he opens the door.

They have some trouble on the way to Paul's apartment, since Ben doesn't know the streets of Brooklyn and Paul isn't used to navigating the city in a car. In the end they have to drive south on Flatbush Avenue, whose long diagonal comprises an extended essay on the borough: bodegas, housing projects, storefront dentists, ethnic hair salons, check cashiers, liquor stores, real estate agencies, discount supermarkets, unused lots, auto body shops, gnarled construction fencing, junkyards. The hellish chaos of traffic at Atlantic Avenue. Walls and windows that over decades have accumulated a dense webbing of spray paint, an intricate knitting of stylized symbols and codes, warnings and boasts.

The presence of his brother makes Paul unusually alert to his surroundings. This is an exotic journey for Ben, who despite his temerity remains a man of caste, and who from day to day doesn't stray from the two poles of his life, home and office. Brooklyn is far-flung territory. Paul knows this not because he asks — they don't speak for the duration of the trip — but because he observes the small, almost surreptitious glances Ben makes out the window, the lines of his forehead traced with something softer than disapproval, a curiosity about what this place is, about where his half-brother has made a life.

Ben relaxes slightly as they drive down the west side of Prospect Park: the blocks of princely brownstones represent a palatable concept of Brooklyn. Ben, whose early impressions of Greenpoint must surely have the faint, benign color of childhood memory, has lived in the city now for decades of his adult life, even longer than Paul, beginning at a time when much of Brooklyn was considered uninhabitable, when even parts of Manhattan were still dangerous. He drives slowly through the roundabout, as if unconvinced of Paul's directions. They make the turn onto his street, empty at this hour. The winter sun is at the end of its dive; the waterline of its shadow has immersed all but the top floors of the west-facing buildings. Ben stops the car.

'This is the place? It's not bad, Paul.'

Paul looks at his brother, who seems sincere. 'Thanks,' he says. 'And for coming to get me. I really hate to make you leave work.'

Ben's face has a hesitant, almost an addled look. 'It was a slow day.'

'How has it — I mean, are you okay?'

'I will be.' Ben pauses. 'It isn't as black and white as the papers like to make it. Parts of their case are shit.'

Paul scratches his throat. It is nearly dusk. 'I should let you go.' When Ben opens his door, he adds: 'You really don't have to come up. I feel fine now.'

'I'm already here.'

He feels an acute reluctance to allow his brother to see his apartment. His head is light, no longer from his condition but from the natural exhaustion at the end of a long day, a long series of days; he craves his own bed, the privacy and certainty there. Yet there's more than fatigue in his unease. It's the problem of gratitude. He's already unsure how to thank Ben for helping him and it would be easier if he left right now, if he hadn't found a willingness – all of a sudden – to play the part of the protective older brother.

At the door, Paul fumbles for his keys, then notices an approaching figure. The man stops and stands at a distance that leaves no doubt of his belligerence. Terence strikes a pose of insolence, vanity, arrogance. Nothing covers the head of trimmed blond hair, a horizon of near-white, a clean incision in the failing light; the hood of a sweatshirt hangs sullenly behind it. His hands are buried deep in his pockets. When he removes one, it has something in its grip; Paul flinches. But Terence has produced only a pack of cigarettes, which he holds outward, as if showing a card. With cool, wiry theater he shakes one free and lights it. The friend from the other night is missing. No one speaks, but Terence stands just within range of the body's intuitive sonar, close enough to play havoc on the animal nerves. Ben obviously feels it too.

Terence can do nothing here, outnumbered and in the open, and he seems to be waiting for someone else to speak. Paul takes a single step in his direction. 'Look,' he begins, in a level tone and, he believes, a sensible one, the much-needed voice of reason. 'Things got out of hand the other night. But I haven't gone to the police. I didn't know that boy and couldn't find him even if I wanted to. I think it would be better if we all just forgot about this.' He can feel Ben behind him, listening to his words, sifting them for an explanation, a narrative; he doesn't speak.

Neither does Terence. He stands, sucking at the cigarette, his posture a little bent now, almost sulking, and were it not for his eyes he wouldn't be especially impressive. His eyes, as dark as chocolate, are the source of his intensity. He aims them directly at Paul.

'I don't know what you want.'

'You talk too much,' says Terence.

Ben has heard all he needs to. He steps forward, so that he stands alongside Paul, who can feel the gravity of his presence, the comfort of it. He speaks crisply. 'I don't know who you are, but you have to go now.' Terence slides his gaze from Paul to Ben. Eyes lock. He takes another drag on the cigarette and wrinkles his nose, a gesture of both disgust and indifference. Ben cascades rapidly into the script, the formal composition, of masculine aggression: 'I said move along.' It is immediately clear that he has an ease in this realm, with the tempo of hostility, that Paul doesn't. He can't help but wonder how Ben, who takes a further step in Terence's direction, would have handled the situation two nights ago. Terence responds with a few paces toward Ben, but hobbles slightly, favoring his right leg. He doesn't speak. Paul senses the rising frustration in his brother, who is accustomed to obedience, especially from someone of Terence's age. Perhaps three feet now separate them; Ben is the larger man. The lit cigarette, pinched between thumb and index finger like a dart, flashes as Terence inhales. His eyes move in sharp flits between the brothers.

'Look at me,' says Ben. 'Not him. I'm the one talking to you now.'

Paul wants to stop his brother, both concerned for his safety and embarrassed at having unwittingly embroiled him in this situation. Ben takes another step. His right hand opens and closes with unspent tension. The space between the two men has become perilously tight.

'I got to see your friend a minute,' says Terence, speaking at last.

'Tell me why.'

'Me and him got some business. Ask him. He knows.'

'I doubt that.'

Terence cocks his head as if to ponder Ben. Then, in a quick, oily motion, as if on a hinge, his arm swings upward, and he looks ready to plant the cigarette's burning root in Ben's face. Paul's innards turn hot and sludgy. But Terence just takes a final drag before killing it on the sidewalk.

'Fine,' he says. 'I'll come back some other time.'

He looks once more at Paul – a strong, slow gaze – then turns and walks in the other direction, fighting to disguise the limp.

Watching until he is out of sight, Paul doesn't move. At last he feels the pressure of his brother's hand against his back, guiding him through the door of the building. They go upstairs. Paul immediately sits, and Ben, who doesn't, moves about warily, stalking along the walls.

'You shouldn't talk to people that way,' Paul says.

'And you shouldn't let some idiot kid bother you like that.'

Ben disappears into the office. Paul can deduce his actions from the sounds they make: turning the pages of a book; rattling the pencils in a cup; knocking his knuckles against the wood of the desk. He calls from the room: 'I take it you're working on something.'

Paul's mind races, afraid that Ben has seen the page about their father – but he put that in a drawer before leaving for the hospital. He answers: 'I've been writing a little about those riots. The ones over the cartoons.' He doesn't know why he lies; perhaps he does so because he can guess that his brother will approve.

'Yeah,' Ben calls back. 'It's awful. Just insane.' He re-appears. 'So are you planning to explain to me what that guy downstairs wanted with you?'

At first, Paul isn't sure that he even wants to tell Ben about what happened. He is exhausted already, sick of it. But as he begins, a desire to talk collects within him, like a broken thing that has begun to repair itself, and the story pours out. He doesn't mention that he was returning home from Claire's. Ben listens patiently. Near the end he walks to the room's other chair and lowers himself into it.

'It's a miracle you weren't killed.'

Paul nods. He has grown used to the communal anxiety, worrying from time to time about nuclear annihilation, that no longer unimaginable decimation of New York, but he can't acclimate himself to this new, more private fear.

He looks out the window, surprised to see that the light is gone. It is still winter – dusk is a blink; night falls at once. Ben speaks.

'That was the hospital, wasn't it, the one where Frank is.'

When Paul doesn't answer, he goes on. 'No one said anything about that; they just explained your condition. That you were fragile. It didn't occur to me until just now, how close you brought me to seeing him.'

'Would it have made a difference,' Paul asks, 'would it have changed anything for you, if Dad – if Frank had apologized?'

Ben looks sharply away, then stands. 'The question is irrelevant,' he says. 'He didn't and he wouldn't have.'

He crosses the room, passing his mute brother on the sofa, until he is right by the door.

'You have no idea what it was like to turn my back on my own father. I was seventeen – think about that. I knew what

I was doing and I knew I had to do it, but there was still no way I could have prepared myself for the feeling of it. I was calm, I remember, when I told Frank that I wasn't going to visit him, not ever again. But then, when I left, it hit me all at once. I was crying.'

He abruptly stops. 'I don't know what you're trying to do,' he says a moment later. 'Why you think I should want to see him. I don't get it, Paul.'

As soon as the words are out he opens the door, then shuts it quietly behind him. From the hall comes the withdrawing sound of footsteps. They are unexpectedly delicate and slow.

Less than an hour after his brother leaves, the phone rings; Paul speaks briefly with a nurse. Nothing is said outright, but he understands what is meant. He calls a car to take him back to the hospital.

On the way he speaks to the funeral director to make the final arrangements; it is not quite six and he catches Wolff at his desk. They will hold the service on Thursday, two days from now – short notice, but the space is available and, as Paul insists, there is no reason to wait. At Wolff's exhort-ation a brief announcement will run in the newspaper tomorrow and on the morning of. Paul has explained once before that such a gesture may be customary but in this particular case is futile, yet as he stares through his own reflection in the car's window at the breeze of passing lights, he hasn't got the energy to renew his objection. Yes, he says. Yes; fine. Publish the notice. You're right, of course. You never know who might turn up.

At the hospital Paul signs some papers without which the body cannot be moved. The nurse explains that he can have as many as two hours before his father is taken to the morgue. Paul won't need nearly so much time, but is glad to know such a thing exists, a customary interval that separates the dead from the living, and gives to each its dignity. At a safe remove, before he must sit in the same room as his father, he toggles the pronouns: he, it. A father is a he, a body is an it. Determining this instant of transformation is no easier than determining the instant life becomes life.

It will be another few minutes before Paul is allowed to see him. Something about preparing the room. Waiting at the nurses' station, he notices a book and picks it up. Heavy. Someone has left a Bible sitting out. The nurse hasn't returned. He strums the pages, thumbing through it backward: an improbable seam in the sea repairs itself; Moses unwisely returns to Egypt. Paul arrives at Genesis, where he finds the story of Abraham and Isaac, whose fascination, in his youth, was primal. He wasn't ever able to place his allegiance with Abraham, where the authors of the Bible want it to be – his imagination offered up too graphic a picture of Isaac's terror. Every time he returned to the story Paul held onto the wish, undiminished by the knowledge of what was to come, that Abraham's hand would stop short of killing his son, not through the intervention of an angel but by its own will. That the selflessness of fatherhood would triumph over the egoism of piety. There's a touch on his shoulder, light, like an insect. He can go in.

The room. The bed. Everything clean, white, straight. It is there, his father's body, though he can't see any difference between it and the thing that has been lying there these past weeks, except for the silence; the machines have been switched off. It is the impersonal hush of a museum or a cathedral. Through the door the nurses watch him, each as they pass, a quick look – quick because to them this isn't an extraordinary sight, a son, a dead father, but it is still a moment that demands a look, even a brief one – and then they are gone, hurrying to attend to different tragedies. Like all temporary figures in life they appear and disappear with breathless speed. Paul stands there for several minutes, minutes that feel like minutes, not unduly long or short. He hardly looks at his father. At one point he considers touching his hand, perhaps holding it, but his own hand refuses to move, paralyzed by the thought of the gesture, by how tender or not tender it would seem, by how cold the skin would be, by the complete absence of sensation in the hand it would be holding, the absence of the possibility of sensation, and Paul knows he can't do even this, perform even this small act of filial tribute, this touch, not for his father, even now that he's dead. God, who isn't there, doesn't care; the nurses, who have troubles of their own, don't care; his father, who is dead, doesn't care. The only one to whom it would matter is Paul, and he cannot lift his hand to touch that of his father's corpse.

He stares at the body and reflects that death is in fact the final limit of the imagination. It is a thought he's had previously. You can imagine another's death — his absence from your life — but not your own; you cannot know what it is like to be a corpse. A corpse has no capacity for thought, desire, or boredom, it has no conception of the future: you cannot truly empty yourself of these things: the imagination isn't strong enough, it cannot cancel itself. When someone speaks of imagining his own death, what he really means is that he has imagined looking at his own dead body, as if from above, which is not at all the same thing.

He first considered death when he was eight or nine. His mother had already been dead for several years, but she existed in an atmosphere of the abstract, of things he took on faith but couldn't see or touch — dinosaurs, his own heart, Russia. He hadn't spent much time contemplating a part of himself that might occupy a realm outside the physical, and upon hearing the word *soul* he pictured a coat with hundreds of pockets, both inside and out, in which you stored all the small treasures you didn't want to lose and, in some cases, meant to keep secret. Once he discovered the fact of death he became obsessed. Everything was death, everything would die. It was so astonishing in its universal application that it failed even to scare him. He can still picture a Civil War battlefield he visited with his father, where he looked out upon endless tides of mist across a field littered with ghosts, where he read the names and dates on monuments. Like all boys he was fascinated by the idea of such violence, such volume of bloodshed. Frank displayed little interest, and it was impossible not to catch his impatience as Paul explored and ran around, his indifference to the things outside his own head. They were driving to Florida, a trip that Frank had announced suddenly and without explanation. Paul was happy to go anywhere that wasn't Brooklyn. On their second day after reaching Florida, Paul's father dressed more sharply than usual, putting on a dark brown suit and taking special care to comb Paul's hair. When Paul asked where they were going, the answer was: 'To pay a visit.'

The house was a dreary two stories, the shingling coming apart all over the roof, and along the shady side were nervy patterns of neglect in the paint, buckling wood, and bent, rusted gutters. It was a house at the end of a slow decline — much like his own, in fact. But there were differences. Corridors of lawn — actual grass — separated this home from its neighbors, and by the front door, in a small planter, bloomed flowers he had never seen.

His father pressed the bell; a woman appeared. She was old, too, but her face had a softness his lacked. She wore her wrinkles more lightly: they were lines traced in sand, not chiseled in stone. Paul studied this unfamiliar figure, but at first she didn't seem to notice him; she looked only at his father.

'I didn't want to show up like this,' his father began. She didn't let him finish.

'Then why did you?'

She was about to say more, then registered Paul's presence. He felt uncomfortable under her gaze, assuming that she found his hair amusing, since to him it looked foolish after his father's ministrations. 'He seems nice,' she said.

They went inside. It was an interior marked by an abundance of soft things: rugs, blankets, pillows. After letting himself be swallowed in a large armchair Paul was given a glass of whole milk. On one side of the room the shelves were stocked with framed photographs. In many he spotted a familiar face, younger than the version he knew but still easily recognized as his older brother. From his perch he surveyed the rest of the house. Clutter didn't dwell in corners, as it did in Paul's home. The piles of newspapers from last year and the year before were nowhere to be found. Pictures were hung, and hung straight. Surfaces were dusted, carpets swept. Someone lived here, and wanted to live here.

But Paul had found himself in the middle of a curious situation: two adults, sitting opposite each other, not saying a word. He was accustomed to his father's silences, but in his experience when you put two grown-ups in a room they usually found something to talk about. This woman and his father weren't even looking at each other.

'Why do you have all the pictures of my brother?'

The woman smiled. She held Paul's eyes, then looked at his father. 'He's very dear, isn't he?'

His father looked at him. Then he turned back to the woman and asked, 'How is Ben?'

'He's got a good job, a very good job.'

'Where's he living?'

The woman stared back at him and said nothing; her face was as expressionless as a plate.

'I just thought—'

'I know what you thought, Frank. But this won't change anything. There's nothing to change.'

'You don't have to talk to me like that. I haven't been here a minute, already you're back at my throat.'

Her eyes filled. 'You brought your own damn throat here for me to get at.'

She paused. 'I understand why you came. I've read your letters. As for Ben . . . it's a shame when a father and a son can't find some common ground. He's a grown man. It's his decision.'

The woman rose from the sofa.

'Look, Paul's finished his milk. I'm glad I could meet him. But you both should go now. I know you've come a long way, but the best thing now is for you both to leave.'

She took the glass from Paul and placed it on the table; then with her thumb she wiped the last chalking of milk from his lip. Together they walked to the front door. Frank, every piece of him hanging in a posture of lethargic surrender, at last stood and followed. At the door the woman put her hand on Paul's head and told him to be good. To his father she said only: 'Goodbye, Frank.' A closed door at their backs, father and son returned to the car without speaking; nor would they speak of that afternoon in the years to come. Paul later had to calculate its significance on his own. He knew only that he'd never seen his father like this; he'd never seen another person cow him into acquiescence. His father had always been a single, unvarying concept, an inscrutable brick of obstinacy and measured silences; now he had another side which had been there all along. Now he was much, much more. Of all that she did, this woman, who even took the care to wipe the milk from his face, was most remarkable for showing him this. The man whose hands now gripped the steering wheel wasn't the man who'd parked the car. Even the sound of Paul's door shutting couldn't be the same as before. The air around him vibrated. His small heart raced.

5

Like she does every morning, she uses her fingernail to burst the dimple on the back of the foil packaging and then to scrape out the small blue pill, which scrambles her hormones and ensures that her body remains uninhabitable. The bed is too hot. She kicks up the covers and spends a moment looking at what they have exposed, her long, naked legs. They seem unnervingly white. Half a glass of water sits on the nightstand, poured maybe a day ago; bubbles climb through it like ivy. Next to her, David is still asleep, and she can hear his soft, tapered breathing. Claire, reaching for the water, sits up, and the sheet slides away from her breasts; with the pill in her mouth and the glass perched on her lips, she looks again at this body beside her own, its hard splinter of collarbone the only fragment visible above the sheet, and cues up a memory from last night. Then she grins, sighs, and swallows.

She's still hot. It has been a long time since she was used to sharing a bed, and she twists away from David, the radiator of another body. Pushing the covers further from her draws them off her companion as well. She lightly touches his stomach. He's slim and well-built, especially for a man in his forties; Paul isn't out of shape, but his body is nothing like David's, which makes her think of a slivered almond, that same soft white, that precision along the edges.

She loves the feeling of him between her legs, his small hips locking into her thighs, the sense of being able to enclose his body, fully, in hers. Comparing his form to Paul's makes her feel guilty, a little mean, as if she's abusing a private reservoir of knowledge. But guilt has a half-life; Paul quickly exits her mind. Her hand, still too gentle to wake this man who is not her husband, grazes downward: she imagines that the backs of her nails are a fine mist against his skin.

Last night they went out. It was Valentine's Day, but that was a coincidence – they hadn't realized the significance of that particular Tuesday when they made the plans. There was dinner, wine. An old-fashioned air of courtship. They ordered a second bottle. And then a glass of port with dessert. She was drunk in the taxi that carried them to her apartment, her thoughts as loose as her hair, the lights of the avenue graphed in blurry lines and dots across her vision. David held her hand. His bones stuck like pebbles between her fingers.

Claire coaxes the sheet down to his waist, then stops. She wonders whether their small account of nights together has given her the right to do more before he wakes. Then she notices that David has an erection, or the beginning of one. Claire looks quickly at his face, but his eyes are closed; he is dreaming. It would be nice if he were dreaming of her. Are they making love behind those eyelids? Feeling greedy, a little reckless, she presses her thighs together, as the particles of desire collect and condense between them, then slowly tugs away the sheet. Once he is in the open she takes him between two fingers, which she moves delicately back and forth, drawing more blood into his penis; she enjoys the feeling of it, its innocent, programmed response. David is uncut. She likes it. The skin at the top is a soft, extra thing, a novel alternative to the others she has seen, where the blood, at the peak of arousal, beats feverishly in the naked bulb.

He is awake. At first she doesn't realize it, mesmerized as she is by the rare, unchaperoned access to this part of a man's body, and when she glances up to find his eyes upon her, she sees that he isn't startled — her attentions, her audacity in waking him like this, have clearly aroused him, and in an instant she feels lust crash through her. She wants everything at once. Removing her eyes from his — she would be embarrassed to watch him watching her — she takes him in her mouth, moving her hand onto the inside of his left leg. The long cords of muscle in his thigh snap tight. A hand reaches through her arms and takes one of her breasts — wild, wanting him, she clasps her hand over his and presses it against her until the tips of his fingers dig into bone. She has him fully, feeling him in the back of her mouth, even using her teeth, and she stops only at the threshold of actual pain, only when his groans turn against her.

Three nights ago she was in this bed, in the same situation, with Paul, although she did not perform this particular act. It has an intimacy, an importance, that sex itself does not. With Paul she simply fucked. With Paul she simply let it happen. At the time it felt natural, and it did not feel bad, but it felt nothing like this now — now she is the one acting, the one whose blood screams to take more, whose heart rings inside her chest.

Her body is an abundance, and it needs his, it needs skin, the contact and tension of muscle. He tugs on a condom. With quick, precise motions she is astride him, she has him, she is working against him; she pounces at his mouth with her own, finds his tongue, bites his lips; she grips his wrists and pins them above his head; she pushes down on his chest for leverage, scuffs her palms against his nipples; she tilts back, feeling a pleasurable strain burn through the muscles that run from her shoulders to her hips, and reaches around to play with his balls; she doesn't know how much noise they make, and doesn't care; she is, she is, she is.

Claire gasps once more, then falls silent. In the shivering aftermath, the merciless accrual of separateness, warmth and lust fall away like dead skin, drift apart like ash, and she becomes cold, recedes into her own head. The explosions of her heart soften, the last, rattling muscles go quiet. She can see clearly again. It is an absent, exhausted feeling, the death of desire.

She pulls the sheet around herself, and then the blanket, noticing that David's eyes, which search her greedily, want her to remain unhidden, his, available for private visual consumption. His gaze touches her as deliberately, as tangibly, as hands. She itches from it and looks away, her own eyes falling upon the nightstand, the empty glass, the package of birth control, the sleeve of cigarettes. For a moment she considers lighting one, but she has promised herself not to do this inside the apartment. Cigarettes just made sense in the months after the divorce, each a handy envelope of pleasure and self-contained guilt, an ideal distraction. She'd smoked on and off in college. In the gnarled logic of heartache and self-pity it felt perfectly natural to adopt a harmful habit. Claire Metzger wasn't a smoker, but that didn't mean that Claire Brennan, following a period of suspended animation, three years off the map, couldn't be.

Paul. It would be unfair to accuse him of anything, not after it was she who asked him up, but he's the one who arrived at her door, and he knew — he knew! — the effect his presence would have. He wanted it to happen. He planned it.

'You're thinking about him,' says David.

'Who?'

'Your ex-husband.'

'Yes,' she admits.

'Good.'

'Good?'

'It means you aren't getting hung up on me.'

He gives a crimped little smile whose meaning is unclear. Is he joking? She hears in his voice the shred of bitterness he can't help. David rolls halfway toward her and possessively touches her bare shoulder; while his touch lingers there her skin revolts, as if it can feel each groove and notch of his fingerprints. What is this inside her? The feeling is intense, private and almost palpable, a physical object materializing within her that she alone has access to. Its value is uncertain. But it gives her one important piece of information: she owes him nothing.

Hastily, she lifts herself from the bed. He doesn't ask where she is going, pretends he isn't staring as she wanders naked through the bright bath of morning. She wants to dress, start the day. In the space of three nights she has slept with two men, one of them her ex-husband, and it troubles her how comfortable she feels within shifting, multiple roles — this isn't a person she wants to be. Indecision seizes her. From next door suddenly comes a familiar sound — a baby's crying, muffled by the wall. She listens. Forgetting the man in her bed, forgetting her own nakedness, forgetting everything, she closes her eyes and strains to hear. After a moment she realizes her mistake. It isn't a child, only the hysterical yelping of channels changing quickly from one to the next. Someone has turned on a television.

Paul goes underground.

From his jacket he retrieves two pieces of paper. One was cut from the newspaper this morning — torn, actually, he didn't take the time to find a pair of scissors – and folded in two. He's read his father's obituary once already, and now peruses it more carefully. An obituary in the newspaper is normally something a family can be grateful for, an exercise in light hagiography; in this case printing one at all seems unfair, even bloodthirsty. It is Paul's fault – the death notice he allowed Wolff to send out must have alerted the newspaper. Even so, he assumed the bar for infamy would be set much higher. His father was hardly James Earl Ray, Lee Harvey Oswald, George Wallace. He wasn't one of the seminal villains of American history; the collective memory has let go. The obituary comes to three paragraphs in length; limns the scope of his father's deeds; notes that he is survived by two sons, both of whom live in New York City and one of whom is Ben Wald, the manager of a hedge fund and currently the subject of a government investigation.

That would be Ben of the solid nuclear family, of the regular visits to a house of worship, of the many colleagues and subordinates, whose years of work in the financial industry have insulated a patiently built life. Even a heart attack can't tear him down. And it is Ben who is the intended recipient of the second piece of paper – an index card addressed on one side with only two pieces of information on the other: the time and place of Frank Metzger's funeral.

It won't do any good; Ben has made that clear enough. He will destroy the card. This morning Paul even tried calling his brother's mobile. Three times; no answer. But he isn't ready to let the occasion pass without his brother knowing that it is going to happen. Ben's arrival at the hospital likely doesn't indicate a change in him, but Paul can't stop himself from wanting it to. Some remnant of the younger brother, in love with the older, is always there.

Eeling out of the tunnel, the train emerges in the light of an aboveground station, and all at once half a dozen people dig phones out of purses, coats, jeans. They snap them open and begin striking the buttons. Paul folds the obituary and slips it back in his pocket with the card. Its importance rests not in who reads it today or who remembers it tomorrow, but in its place in the public record, proof of its enduring truth, baked forever into the labyrinth of searchable databases in which all the world's knowledge now resides, cities of hard drives buried underground, hot, humming, and smug.

At the apartment, he studies himself in the mirrors that panel the elevator and, feeling a familiar displeasure at his own appearance, exits the lift to find Beth standing in the door frame.

'Is Ben home?'

She pauses. 'No – it's Wednesday, Paul. It's a weekday. Is everything all right?'

'Can I come in?'

Beth deposits him in the living room and returns with two steaming mugs of coffee. He accepts one and without taking a sip lowers it onto the glass-top table, careful not to let a drop escape, then promptly forgets about it. Beth holds hers with two hands, dearly, like a reliquary. She sits opposite him, her back straight, her demeanor wooden. She's a proper-looking woman, dressed in slacks and a pale blue sweater; her silvering brown hair is cut just above the shoulders. The difference in their ages is great enough that Paul can't help but think of her as maternal – having never known his own, he has a habit of seeking out temporary mothers. He has always been comfortable in her presence. Beth's eyes blink rapidly, especially when she listens to another person speak, and their arrangement, set far apart, accentuates an unusual size and gentleness.

Paul takes out the card and, handing it to Beth, says: 'I don't mean to intrude. I just came to give this to Ben.'

She stares at it. 'I'll make sure he gets it.' She adds, quickly and quietly, 'I'm so sorry, Paul.'

That concludes their business. But he hasn't had his coffee, and, oddly, he doesn't want to go. The good order of things, the cleanliness, the brightness, make Paul want to stay; it feels so remote from his own apartment, the life he's allowed to collect around him, the loneliness there, the congealed silences. He reaches for his coffee and sucks up two abrupt sips before asking: 'How's Jake?'

Beth smiles gratefully. 'He's good. He's a sophomore now.'

'Ben told me.'

'He was thinking of majoring in economics, but his father wants Jake to study history or philosophy, something like that. He wants a college professor for a son.'

Paul finds the idea almost humorous, Ben discouraging his son from becoming a hardhearted businessman like he is. He wants to be a good father, the kind of father they didn't have – a thought that makes Paul admire his brother, in a roundabout way, though it can't help but sadden him a little, too.

'And what do you think?'

'I think Jake should do whatever makes him happy.'

Strange to remember that he once knew his nephew as a baby – a little tablet of possibility, bonelessly soft, made easily glad by the most mundane trinkets of the world. This was back when he was not quite twenty and Ben tolerated the occasional visit. It has been years. Paul wonders what kind of man his nephew has become. Surely he's tall, strong, and in full bloom, exhibiting his father's many physical gifts. Confident and well-liked. Ben wouldn't have any other kind of son.

He asks, 'Is Ben going to be all right?'

For what seems like a long time she doesn't answer. When she does speak, her sentences are broken by long, uneven pauses. 'He's never not been all right before. What they say about him — it's hard to take. The issues aren't ones I really understand. Ben hasn't been himself. It hasn't been easy. I don't know.'

'You don't talk to him about it?'

'We talk about other things. With all this going on, Ben's been concentrating on other things. Family. Temple. He's on the phone a lot with Jake.'

Holding the coffee mug, Paul stands and begins to walk slowly around the room. It is a little chilly and for the first time he notices that the sweater his sister-in-law wears is quite heavy. He moves toward the glass shelves, ornamented with photographs.

He looks at a picture of Ben and Beth with a woman he doesn't recognize, but who could be Beth's sister. He says, 'I always wondered if you asked Ben to convert before you married him.'

She makes a quizzical face. 'No, not at all. It was his idea, actually. And once he gets going . . . My father had a brother who married outside the faith. Someone on my mother's side, too, I think. We weren't that kind of family. I was in love. I would have married him no matter what.'

Paul glances out the window at the clutter of buildings in the distance. 'I didn't mean to pry.'

She says, 'It always surprised me.' Paul looks at her. 'The strength of his faith, I mean. Maybe it's always that way, if you convert to a religion instead of growing up with it. Maybe it belongs to you in a way I don't understand.'

'He insisted on converting.'

'It's funny. I think that over the years my own faith has grown stronger because of him. I think differently about

God. He's made me more serious about Judaism. More serious about all of it, I suppose.'

She grows silent, her expression like that of a woman snapping shut her purse to prevent a stranger from seeing inside. The reason for Paul's visit has drifted away during their conversation, but the present silence offers no resistance, and it returns, poisoning the air between them.

'Let me warm you up.' Beth takes his coffee, which Paul has barely touched, and heads for the kitchen.

'I should go, actually.'

Beth stops and nods. There isn't an established ritual for parting from his sister-in-law; they have had too few opportunities. He wavers, unsure if he's supposed to embrace her, and then realizes that because of the two mugs in her hands it would, in any case, be impossible.

On his way back to the subway, Paul passes a row of white news vans waiting along the street like ambulances. The locus of interest seems to be one of the apartment buildings on West Eighty-second Street, perhaps a private disgrace made newsworthy by the identity of one of its principals. It could be a death. In any case, nothing is happening at the moment, and the only activity on the block is a reporter, dressed in a suit, having a cigarette and jawing with the cameraman.

He could have left the city after his divorce. Nothing holds him here; he could have gone anywhere. The work he does is moveable. Other cities are inexpensive, intimate, uncrowded; they have different seasons, new people, unfamiliar streets. He could have gone to San Francisco. He could have gone to a place like Denver or Minneapolis, one of those smaller cities in the middle of the country routinely praised as 'livable' – able to be lived in. Is he able to live here? People often leave after a personal loss; people will move out of grief. Then again, those same things can make people stay put. He has never thought of leaving, not seriously. Not even to pursue one of the old post-college dreams, taking up life as an expatriate, in Amsterdam, Budapest, Buenos Aires. Berlin is supposedly cheap these days.

They are tearing down a building on West Seventy-second Street. He looks inside, through its stripped face, at floors where workmen carefully pull back unwanted beams and pieces of stone. Pink, fluffy insulation swells in the gaps like an infection. The building is being remodeled then, not torn down; the destruction moves too slowly for a demolition. He gets on the subway, gets off.

Who would he tell, if he left?

He stands on Madison Avenue. Paul hasn't been this busy in weeks, even months. Fresh from delivering the card to Beth, he now has a meeting, arranged on short notice, with this editor, Bentham, a man whom as little as forty-eight hours ago he firmly intended never to see again. He dislikes Bentham and knows that a second encounter won't change that. But earlier today, in the period of clarity that often follows sleep, he sat for a long time, drinking coffee and staring out the window, only vaguely aware of the movement of buses and people, and made a decision.

It would be good, Paul came to think, if this morning's obituary were not the last comment on his father's life committed to the public record. A book of the kind Bentham has proposed wouldn't, in and of itself, constitute an act of disloyalty; it would all depend on how he handled the material.

And there lay a second idea — Ben. Without fully understanding the charges facing his brother, Paul recognizes how much worse it has been made by the past the newspapers have exhumed: Ben Wald, né Metzger, a practicing Jew no less, is the son of a Nazi. It fits the picture they want. One buried secret stands as proof of others. Even Paul feels a growing sense of umbrage at this turn of events. He cannot judge Ben's innocence or guilt, although it isn't hard to imagine his brother forcing the system to abide by him instead of the reverse — but that isn't the point. Using their father was shameless. The papers have erased forty years of tireless effort. No matter what his crimes, Ben has earned the right not to be a Metzger.

A book about their father would give Paul the opportunity to make this fact loudly known, to pump it into the public chambers of information. He may be deluding himself. But if there is a chance to have his brother understand that he doesn't judge him for turning his back on their father, that though he doesn't agree with it he recognizes the integrity in it, then perhaps Ben will soften his own judgment of Paul for not doing the same. In print it might be possible — mightn't it? — to revise the terms of their brotherhood by making Ben a figure of sympathy: a man of highest principle who made a terrifying choice, at the cost of his own father, because it was the only one he felt was right.

And if Bentham isn't lying, or irrationally optimistic, this book could restore a basic aspect of dignity to Paul's life. It could sell. He could, more than notionally, be a writer. In time he could move out of his lonely apartment, his distant neighborhood, into somewhere brighter, fuller, busier. In time he could even afford to live in Manhattan. Would it impress Claire? It seemed until recently that his chances were gone. He would have to be truly mad to reject, on the basis of a vague, shifting principle, the only one that has come along in years.

An assistant takes Paul immediately to Bentham's office. He is sitting behind the desk, writing in an appointment book.

'I've reconsidered your offer,' says Paul after the editor invites him to sit.

'It seems so.' There's a hard, sharp glint suspended in the back of Bentham's eye, like something frozen in thick ice. 'What changed your mind?'

'That isn't important. All you need to know is that I'll do it.'

The editor smiles and, in mock deference to Paul's show of hostility, puts up a pair of open palms.

'When we last met, you said this would be my book.'

'I did.'

'No swastikas on the cover. Nothing tasteless.'

'Yes.'

'And you'll publish it, this book, however I choose to write it?'

'There will have to be a certain measure of editorial discretion, of course.'

'I want you to know that I'm agreeing to this only with serious misgivings.'

The editor pauses and, leaning toward Paul, joins his hands in an arrow, aimed directly across the desk.

'I would say you've made that awfully clear.'

He waits for a large, threshing pack of schoolchildren to cross over before having the bar code on his own ticket scanned. They rush ahead like swallows down the roped corridor that admits entrance to the museum, as their teacher makes a futile pursuit, calling for them to hush down, to respect the place they're in. A second teacher lags reluctantly behind; he is younger and seems faintly embarrassed by it all. Paul sees a guard grin. By the time he finds them again in the main hall, whose ceiling reaches far enough above them to achieve the distance and abstraction of sky, the teacher has regained control of her students.

They remember what she surely told them before arriving: this is a museum, not a playground; the works of art here are priceless, or at least worth millions of dollars; you are to keep your voices down, walk at a reasonable pace, and, above all, you are not to touch anything. The students each clutch a black-and-white composition notebook.

It is a field trip, a chance to force-feed culture to ten-year-olds. He remembers these from his own childhood in Brooklyn, the voltage of an excursion to Manhattan, then as much an idea as a place; Frank never took him, never saw the point — Manhattan was more buildings, more people, more noise, more construction, more car exhaust, more assholes and criminals and deadbeats and drunks. Paul would prefer not to analyze his reasons for being here now. He's visited this museum dozens of times, but not since the divorce. Elsewhere in the building, Claire is at work, sitting at a desk or walking around the office as she speaks on the phone; she isn't down in the galleries, among people. She won't see him. Feeling a pungent sense of displeasure after meeting with Bentham again, he came here: he can purchase a ticket like anyone else and with that, the price of admission, have the run of the museum. It is a public place.

In the atrium he spots a series of four abstract paintings by Cy Twombly. They are among Claire's favorites; he didn't know they had come to New York. Behind him two of the children dart past like rabbits, jostling his coat. A clutch of five girls, gossips, loiter nearby, giggling and writing in their notebooks. They don't look at the art. Elsewhere the younger, male teacher sternly addresses a group of boys. Despite the teachers' efforts, the volume of chatter swells and fills the enormous hall. There are perhaps thirty kids in the room, caroming around the floor like pool balls. Finding it difficult to concentrate on the paintings in front of him, Paul moves to the next room, the gallery of contemporary art. Big things. Found objects. Video. Industrial materials, manipulated photographs, looping words of lurid pink neon.

Claire knows how to look at such things, and how to speak intelligently about their intent; he has always had trouble. These frictionless surfaces offer no traction. Although he has no formal training, Paul has long felt entitled to his opinions of art, as someone who has spent so much time around it. He and Claire share a love of earlier artists, or they once did, of the postwar generation, the abstract expressionists, de Kooning and Johns, and the artists before them, the clearly marked trail going back – Picasso, yes, and also Giacometti, Schiele, the German expressionists, and then Munch, Vuillard, Rodin, Manet. They both admire Cézanne. Claire knows more, has an internal library of images a thousand times the size of his own, but at heart she likes what he likes. Together they saw dozens of museums – and it has never occurred to him with quite such immediacy that he's been conditioned to look at art with her, to anticipate Claire's opinions and to have her nearby to offer his own. He hasn't visited a single museum since the divorce; the last ten months are perhaps the longest he's gone in his adult life without setting foot inside one. He feels the build-up of unexpressed thoughts like a stuck vein inside his head and looks more than once to his right, his mouth already beginning to form a word, as if she will be there to hear it.

Trapped in these thoughts, he isn't looking at the art in front of him. If his eyes focus long enough to notice anything, it is his own fading reflection in the glass of the frame, and the reflections flickering behind him, a room's worth of bodies, fragmented and floating back and forth. In this tableau, at the center of which hangs his own face, he notices another's: a woman's, her features obscured but her figure familiar, familiar enough; she stands at about the right height, with the right length of hair, with a similar style of dress.

He turns – she's already moving toward a sculpture in the middle of the floor. He doesn't follow at once. When he does, he selects an indirect course, standing not beside her at the sculpture, but at a piece on the opposite side of the room; once again, he isn't really looking, rather using the glass of the frame as a mirror, a way to pick out her movements, which surely gives the impression of staring all the more intensely at the art itself. She stands at the sculpture for a long time, then walks away, out of the room. Paul dithers, makes up his mind. He goes after her.

The main hall again. Most of the children have gone. Three kids blast across one of the exposed catwalks of the upper galleries. A call echoes down.

She's looking at the paintings Paul stopped by earlier, the sequence of four, each one a season; she stands at the first, at spring, and Paul, preserving a certain distance, begins at the end, with winter, although his eyes focus on the piece immediately to his left. *Autunno*. Vermilion, magenta, brown, and black, purples and yellows, all erupt in bursts and shocked splotches, and in fat, longitudinal drips that run almost to the bottom; in places the brush strokes are so thick that the paint burbles off the canvas, hangs there in gnarled, gristly threads. From elsewhere he hears a guard's tired remonstrations: 'No flash. No flash.' In the outermost parenthesis of his vision he sees her advance from spring to summer. The resemblance is uncanny.

A figure steps between them – a small girl. She looks eight or nine, perhaps too young to be part of the school group, although Paul isn't good at guessing ages, and upon approaching the painting, *Autunno*, she squeezes her face into a quizzical pouch. The piece gives her no grip, no figure for her to wrap her imagination around, no scene for which to invent a narrative. It is simply color and blank space, absence and presence, a grisly convulsion. She stares. The woman, Paul notices, now looks away, as if deciding where to go next.

Paul is about to turn as well when he sees that the young girl's finger, inches from the canvas and extended in an innocent gesture of indication, hasn't stopped moving; then, without the hesitation that would suggest an aware-ness of the inherent transgression, it is touching the artwork, penetrating what seemed impenetrable. The canvas bends like a mattress. She picks briefly at a particularly thick clot as at a scab, before she pulls away her hand and then, as if nothing has happened, leaves. Paul's mind is fixed on the sight. It has the visceral shock of a finger pressing against the wet, purple bulge of an exposed brain. No one else saw what took place, no alarms were triggered, none of the guards was watching. Whatever now bristles inside of him recalls the first sensations as he approached the two men beating the boy, but more concentrated, all that violence shrunk to the tip of a small girl's index finger.

Even as he finally turns away and, catching a glimpse of the woman just as she leaves the main hall, quickly follows her out, Paul feels an unfamiliar chemical elation from what he saw. The crowds are growing. Tourists chatter like magpies. A glutted escalator carries them to the third floor. His thoughts still blink with a strobing flutter; the image of the girl's finger touching the canvas holds his mind like a startling piece of pornography. He manages not to lose the woman. Briefly she and Paul are in the architecture wing; he pretends to look at a photograph of a Soviet-era housing complex. Half the windows are broken. A French couple behind him seem much more interested by it than he is, and he stands aside to allow them a closer look. When she leaves he waits a beat, then makes his own exit.

In the fourth-floor galleries the pace slows. At certain pieces she hovers: one of Pollock's hypnotic, wiry nests; a baboon howling with terrific pain; a giant abstract canvas, covered in tarry black, with only a few spills of color, a hatching of blood and yolk. Fluorescent lights of different lengths slatted into a bright cathedral: his eyes hurt when he stares at it. Paul preserves a steady distance between himself and the woman, but enjoys, after she has walked away, trying to retrieve, in the air, a residue of her thoughts, a fiber of emotion. He avoids a clean view of her face, observing her only in sidelong glances, slivers of profile, nothing his eye can hold onto. It ensures also that she doesn't see him. He lets her chart the course. Occasionally someone speaks too loudly in one of the galleries and breaks his reverie — it is always a woman, middle-aged, from out of town. Around him footsteps scuff and slap the hardwood floor.

He can admit now that she bears little resemblance to Claire. With every glimpse of her face, even fragments and flashes of it, the knowledge ossifies; he knows she isn't his wife, she isn't even a close match. Yet this awareness doesn't diminish his enthusiasm: he follows more closely, and more carelessly.

Things thicken considerably in the room of Picassos. People press toward him with the peculiar intimacy of the art museum; they bump his shoulder while trying to read a title card or examine a brush stroke. In the jostle of heads, it takes Paul a moment to realize that she's already come and gone. He spots her in the far doorway, the back of her, and pushes through. By the time he reaches the next room, she is nowhere to be found.

Slowly and mindlessly he follows the escalators back down to the main hall. To his surprise she is there, standing once more in front of the Twombly paintings, framed by the enormous white wall. As he halts beside her — they are standing in front of the last piece: *Inverno* — she senses his presence and turns slightly. They smile. Now that he can see her face directly he understands how foolish this has been. He feels faintly ashamed.

She moves her eyes from him to the paintings. 'You seem to really love these,' she says. He must look nonplussed, because she adds: 'Earlier. You were staring at them so intently.'

She has been aware of him, too.

He nods. 'I've always found this one a bit terrifying.'

They look together at the hazy black orb sinking through the dun canvas: it suggests not only the end of a given year, the frozen passages of winter, but the onset of a greater, more grievous finale. In its dying sun it is easy to imagine that Twombly had in mind a much more permanent descent.

'It surprised me,' she says, 'how quickly he turns from something lovely to something so dark and — yes, so terrifying.'

He says, 'I once saw them in London with my wife.'

She gives him a strained smile, and both turn back to the painting. After a suitable interval, she wanders away, pauses at the piece on the opposite side of the room, and then vanishes down the stairs in the direction of the museum's exit.

Paul lowers himself onto a bench. He wasn't following this woman but Claire, a fantasy of proximity, and into the space he has allowed a stranger to occupy for the past hour now seep memories of his wife.

When the end of their marriage perhaps had become inevitable, he and Claire went to Venice. It was a vacation not only from home but from marriage itself: the weight, the accretion of silence, the litany of grievances. Months later they would be divorced. But for a week they were happy: they ate long dinners and had conversations that reminded Paul of their first year; they took walks through the city and spent hours in the museums, holding hands and talking about the art; after staring at an erotic canvas by Modigliani they even snuck into a bathroom to make love. Claire threw pennies into fountains, laughed at herself for trusting in wishes. Their voices climbed the egg-brown walls of empty squares. Venice encased them in the unfamiliar, made them residents of their own private ambit. Like anonymous lovers they devoured the city and each other; no whim passed unindulged. The versions of themselves who were unhappy in marriage, who were charting a slow path toward its demise — those unfortunate people were back in New York, stewing glumly in their apartment, chewing bitterly on the silence. Meanwhile, in Venice, Paul made a cuckold of himself, taking every chance to touch Claire, to bite down on a mouthful of her flesh and hold it between his teeth.

In the afternoons they would nap after making love. At some point he'd wake, or she would, and they would loll in bed like buoys, touching and parting without pattern or purpose. Minutes would collect with a satisfying sense of time accumulating rather than passing. On one such afternoon, rolling over and looking at him through eyes clotted with sleep, she mumbled: 'Isn't this like a movie? Can't you imagine us in black and white right now?'

She spoke again. 'I love the sound of bodies in bed.

In films now there's never enough silence. They never let a moment breathe. I love older movies. They used to listen. Skin against sheets – I love that sound. I want our movie to have that. No talking, no soundtrack.'

Then: 'Hotel bedsheets are always so crisp – they're perfect for that.'

He pinched the fabric and worked it between his fingers. She rolled away again so that he couldn't see her face. Without warning a feeling of inexpressible sadness filled his heart; he felt the room close around them, a hotel room in a foreign city, with its unfamiliar habits of light, its narcotic air of freedom. A temporary place.

Paul, whose eyes have been shut now for a long time, opens them only with reluctance, finding it difficult to observe others' faces, their smiles, even children's looks of boredom. His father is dead. It's been hours since he considered that new fact. He checks his watch – he doesn't have anywhere to be, but he ought to go. Why did he come here? Why did he pretend that being here, in rooms full of art that he has seen with his wife, in the building where she works, wouldn't have exactly this effect on him? The muscles in his legs flex as if to stand, yet he can't. Memory, as painful as it can be, is addicting.

In their third year, after the fighting had exhausted them, silence pushed into the marriage. Both left it unaddressed, seeming to think it would pass if they gave it time, and grateful, certainly, for a return to calm. Paul spent more hours in his office, a small room at the end of the hall; every week another friend of Claire's from college turned up, requiring a long evening out, at the end of which she would come home half drunk, chatty and brightly oblivious to Paul. Sex was infrequent. Eventually the silence came to seem like a piece of furniture that had been around too long to get rid of. At the very end the pressure that had built within the walls of the apartment abated. Both knew what was coming; both had adapted to the inevitability of divorce. It actually became easier. They were gentler with one another. They learned that divorce, like marriage, has a rhythm. They grew comfortable with the silence, used to the oppressive, dewy emotion that clung to everything in the apartment, to the upholstery, the dinner plates, the drapes — if it can be said that you get used to it, to that kind of sadness.

6

Paul has only a light headache, but swallows three aspirin, then decides it would be better to have four. In the hours that follow he molders in the apartment, tired but not asleep. The light changes first to a sultry gray and then finally to black. After it has been dark for a long time he stumbles from the sofa, lurching into the room. It responds with a mirthless chatter of creaks and groans; an empty room is always louder than a fully furnished one. His apartment is a study in absences: no bed, no dining table, no place to sit other than the sofa. The end of his marriage swept away many of his possessions, and along with them the urge to acquire new ones.

So few people even know he's here. The mailman, who sees his name along the bottoms of magazine covers; Ben, who was forced by circumstance to visit. Credit card companies, the gas and electric conglomerates, who remember him in their databases. It occurs to Paul that he hasn't even bothered to write his name on the list of tenants by the front door. Rashly, he rattles around the room in search of a pen, finally finding a cheap ballpoint on the windowsill; then, pulling on his jacket, he jogs downstairs, intending at least to affix his name to his place of residence. Outside the cold bangs into him; with frozen, ungloved fingers, he pries up the plastic cover that shields the tenant list. Against his apartment number he sees the name of the previous occupant. He uncaps the pen and tries to cross it out. Nothing happens – the pen is dry. He works it against the card until the nib scrapes through entirely, mutilating the paper and leaving a sordid gash. Paul lets the pen fall to the cement, where it gives a tepid double tap. He starts to reach for his keys, then stops: the thought is dismal, going back upstairs, returning to an apartment where no one even knows he lives.

Instead he walks toward the cafe, though he can't remember if it's even open at this hour. Once, he has the feeling that someone is behind him, but when he turns there's no one there; even so, he's relieved to find the lights still on at the cafe. A few more steps and he can even see Pirro, slanted over a mop he pushes from one end of the window to the other, then back again.

'You're just in time,' Pirro says when Paul walks in. 'I am about to close.'

Without asking for Paul's order, he goes behind the counter and makes a coffee, the largest size.

'All right if I sit here for a little?' asks Paul, taking the paper cup.

'Sure, sure. It will take me thirty, forty minutes to clean up anyway. And you are a friend. You are always welcome.'

Paul tastes the coffee, recoiling when a little dark wave leaps clumsily over the lip of the cup and scalds him.

'Do you mind the radio?'

Pirro is already working the dial. From the static emerges a crisp British accent. 'I hate American music,' he says. 'I put on the news. Just to have something to listen to.'

The report is an assortment of the usual. Taking tender sips of the coffee, Paul concentrates on it briefly, then lets his mind slip; Pirro isn't paying attention at all. He puts his weight behind the mop's stem, urging it forward, peeling away a strip of glistening checkered floor. He's halfway done when something in the newscast catches his interest. 'What a bitch. I can't believe they did not hang her.'

'Who?'

'Oh, you know, that woman. The one with a country for a name. England.'

On the radio is a discussion about the modern use of images, how the shocking becomes banal. The host has just mentioned Abu Ghraib: the horrid, hooded man, his arms outstretched as if hanging on the cross, wires dripping from his hands like threads of blood. How rapidly, says the host, it became canonical, like the *Mona Lisa*, ready for mass production on T-shirts and wall posters. She goes on to cite other enduring images of arrested death: the Spanish partisan, shot in battle, flailing back; the bullet passing through the head of a Vietnamese man; someone dropping from the World Trade Center like a blurry branch.

'Women just aren't supposed to be like that,' Pirro adds.

Paul nods, not knowing what else to say: no, women are not supposed to be like that. Nor, he thinks, are men, although perhaps he is wrong about that, and cruelty – bodily cruelty – is written into every masculine life. He takes his coffee to the window and stares blankly at the street. A few cars make quarter- and half-circuits through the roundabout. On the other side is the cinema, whose marquee holds a brilliant white vigil, but from here Paul can't make out the titles of the films it advertises. His eyes change focus. In the center of the roundabout is a pedestrian island. A person is standing there, at its near edge. There are bushes and benches on which vagrants sleep, but this is not a vagrant. At first the figure seems to be a trick of vision, the result of zooming between distances too quickly. Eyes are especially unreliable at night, and it's difficult to see through the yolky puddles of light on the windowpane, through the ghost of his own reflection. He concentrates. He is certain there was someone there, even if now he's gone.

'Listen,' says Pirro, oblivious to Paul's unease, 'I always have a beer while I clean up. No one minds. You want one?'

When Paul finally turns from the window, he sees Pirro, the mop leaning into his ribs like a rifle stock, already flexing the caps off two brown bottles. He doesn't notice as Paul replies, 'Yes. Yes, why not.'

After going through the day's mail his first act is to fill a tumbler with ice and a generous amount of Scotch. He waits for the drink to settle, listening to the liquor sizzle and crack as it finds pockets of air in the ice and they burst. Ben hasn't bothered to turn on the light in the study. He wants to have his drink in darkness. This is a celebration, a private one. As the clear strong flavor rises into the back of his nose, he holds the first sip on his tongue, suppressing the urge to swallow it immediately. Ben has always enjoyed little games of willpower, in which he competes only against himself; the Scotch runs down his throat. He replaces the glass on the desk, using the card his brother left as a coaster.

His wife walks up behind him. 'Do you want company?'

Yesterday, almost the whole of which he spent in the apartment, the monotony broken only by the trip to the hospital to pick up Paul, drove him crazy. This morning he had to get out, and he went early, before his wife was awake, in search of sunshine, oxygen, activity, distraction; he went without his mobile phone. For the whole day he walked all over the city, gulping it down like a tourist. Streets he'd never seen. Men performing drum music in a square. High, thin clicks chattering above a deep, violent pulse. Sounds born in a far-flung part of the world – there was a primal, tribal, even a sexual energy to it, a brutal, warlike dissonance. It rang in his blood. He imagined it as music used to rouse men for a slaughter. He had difficulty pulling himself away; he watched for half an hour, wrapped in his coat, then ate at a small cafe. No one looked at him. Beth's presence should calm him, ease him back to a feeling of normalcy, but his agitation isn't so easily solved. She's been worried about him, she knows the weight of everything that has piled up. His brother. His father. Work – the absence of it, the rest of the world continuing to operate without his hands on the levers. His wife's concern is understandable.

The silence hangs too long. 'So,' his wife says, 'what have you been doing all day?'

'Nothing. I took a walk.'

'I didn't even realize you were gone until Paul came by. I assumed you were just in your study.' When he says nothing, she adds, 'We said we would have lunch.'

'I had a sandwich at this little place.'

At the cafe he read the papers cover to cover, both the *Times* and the *Journal*, and watched the people at other tables. Young men, a few women, typing on laptop computers. Ears plugged with small, uncomfortable-looking headphones. They smiled periodically, laughed to themselves. He left, wondering what to do. Yesterday Beth had suggested that he read a book. She meant a novel; he hates fiction. It put the idea in his head nonetheless, and he walked to the bookstore on Eighty-sixth Street, intending to purchase a new biography of Eisenhower he'd read about, but it was out of stock. He walked around a while longer, sat by the lake in Central Park, and then finally came home, where he slipped in quietly and found the card on his desk.

'Beth. Please. I just need a moment to myself.' She leaves without another word. The floorboards groan under her feet, the usual murmurs, the brooding of a building with history.

Left alone, he takes another delicate swallow of the Scotch.

His lips shrink with the pleasurable sting of ice. He hasn't been to work in two days, but the work lives within him, the numbers, hunches, pressures, the anxiety like a vapor in his chest. Energy futures have been especially volatile. Flux is worrying. Markets prefer constancy. There's another hostage situation in Nigeria's oil fields. Politics are obstructing development in Russia. He runs his thumb along the edge of the desk, trying to hush his mind. The desk is a good, solid piece, one hundred percent walnut; he bought it years ago, a gift for himself, a piece of furniture that fitted his idea of who he was and would become.

There's also Paul to think of. It's not worth being angry at him for leaving the card, even if the trace of fraternal provocation is unmistakable. He wanted to accuse Ben one last time of the crime of rejecting their father, maybe make a last effort to persuade him to relent on the matter of the will; in consenting to retrieve his brother from the hospital, perhaps Ben had made too large a gesture, one open to misinterpretation. He still isn't sure why, when she asked yesterday where he was going, he felt the need to lie to his wife about the errand.

His brother doesn't know the full story. Paul only knows that he, Ben Wald, turned his back on their father. Paul wasn't even born then. He doesn't understand that Ben did, once, love his father, as all boys do. That he was confused by his parents' divorce – in an era when that was far less common – and even more so by the silence with which his mother plastered over it: she allowed him to see Frank but never spoke of him, and always got tight when his name came up. Paul doesn't know how those years twisted up Ben, how they gnarled his insides, how they slowly made him hard. Ben knew his mother had been hurt by Frank but didn't know why or how. He learned from her a method of living: when you leave, you leave; you don't speak of the thing you left. And yet he did not hate his father – certainly he didn't want to. He wanted only what any boy wants: affection, instruction, praise. Frank tried, Ben knows; he did. Like so many divorced fathers he attempted to fatten their lean hours together with meaning and trust. When Ben visited him Frank was attentive, if guarded; were Ben to let himself recall them, the small moments would add up: being handed the razor and then shaving his father's face for him, even after nicking him on the chin; eating bland meals of chicken and rice as Frank studied him for signs of enjoyment; suffering Frank's inquiries, delivered with pretended casualness, about his mother. But there was a cavity, and when Ben learned the truth – of who his father was – it didn't even come as a surprise. Of course, he thought. Of course there's something more. The reluctant submission to his father's restrained affection turned to disgust under the pressure of those greedy, self-pitying eyes. From Frank, who had given him so little, he was now determined to take nothing at all. He used the fact of his father's past and took shape around it, like an oyster with its pearl. He used it to make himself and then, at seventeen, he acted. The choice defines him. Ben is the Ben only who did this, who broke free. Frank was a poor father because he had already failed inexorably as a human being. And that is what Paul doesn't understand. Paul, who has endured none of it, who wouldn't have had the strength, and who doesn't know what it means to destroy a part of yourself. Ben sawed and chiseled until the idea became truth: there existed no one whom he could call Father, or Dad, or any of the names people use. He effaced the concept from his emotional lexicon. It formed again only when Jake was born. How could Paul understand that? Who isn't even a father. How could Paul understand that each time his son addresses him – 'Dad' – there rises up in Ben an extra, shivering throb of pleasure and pride, almost painful in its strength, one which must exceed that of even the most devoted and loving parents?

He stands. His blood shakes a little. The Scotch wasted no time working its way under his skin; drinking has become a rare event, especially with his heart. His mouth feels dry, and he squeezes his tongue against the roof. Arguing with Paul in his head will get him nowhere. Ice, still melting and restless, knocks around the glass. Steadying himself against the door frame, he pauses, then makes his way to the living room.

She doesn't see him yet: sitting on the sofa, she dips her head over a book, her neck curved like a swan's, and a few strands of hair fall toward the page. Girlishly, she has tucked one leg under herself, halfway into a lotus position. Beth has a trick of folding into herself that he loves. Nothing in the world but the sight of his wife can make him feel this sense of calm, comfort, completion.

'I bet you think I should go to the funeral,' he says.

She looks up and smiles, surprised, her eyes animated by a glitter of concern. 'Your brother seemed on edge. As though something were wrong. Something else, I mean.'

'It's probably nothing.'

He thinks of the kid outside his brother's apartment. Ben is a man who appreciates risk, the value of partial information, and he knows when he doesn't have enough. But it seems implausible that Paul got mixed up in such grim business – for one thing, his account of the dust-up in the street certainly contained a grain of exaggeration – and yet the one Ben saw did have a hardness in his eyes, an uncommon determination. Still, it's hard to believe that he plans to come around again. Characters like him have short attention spans; he'll find someone else to bother.

'Maybe you could talk to him.'

'Which do you want me to do? Talk to Paul? Or go to my father's funeral?'

'Ben.'

It can mean many different things, his own name. In this case, it has buried within it a gentle accusation of brotherly responsibility. During the first half of their marriage she leaned on him to include Paul in their lives. Time and again he acquiesced. It was she who made Ben invite him to their son's bar mitzvah. He wishes now that he hadn't lied to her about going to the hospital; he almost never keeps secrets from his wife — only those which are absolutely in her best interests. It's too late to tell her now. In any case, he isn't sure what he would tell her — that he can sense a decrease within himself of resolve; it began after a week of seeing his father's name alongside his own in the papers, when Paul came to see him on Sunday morning.

It may turn out to be nothing more than a stray product of the emotional untidiness he has felt since his son started college, which in time he will learn to control as he finds other vents for the surplus affection he's been left with. And it has nothing to do with his convictions about Frank. He'll continue to hold them, especially if he consents to a version of brotherhood: he must keep his grip on the firm thing, the thing he understands best, the one thing that has always been there. That can't be undone. His younger brother isn't going to undo it.

His wife's voice, again.

'I think you might not realize you regret it until it's too late.'

'I'm old enough to know what I will and won't regret.' He didn't intend it to come out that way — it leapt from his mouth — and he manages to force the beginning of a smile. He says: 'I just can't. I'd rather spend the day with you.'

'You'd better not try to charm me after your disappearing act this morning.'

'Want company?'

'Always.'

'Let me get my drink.'

He disappears from the room and returns to the study. To his eyes, accustomed now to the lights of the living room, the darkness is impossibly inky. He doesn't bother to turn on the lamp and instead feels his way to the desk, inching through the familiar space, stubbing his toe against the leg of a chair and breathing a single oath. He retrieves what's left of his Scotch, but doesn't yet turn to leave.

After the heart attack, during his recovery as he lay on the hospital bed – in a private room with a view of Manhattan as fine as that from many of the city's boardrooms and hotels – Beth and Jake sat with him. He breathed heavily, and never had much to say, but they stayed; they stayed while he slept. This was more than a year ago. On the second day, Jake had to go back to school and Beth left for several hours, and he recalls those hours as the worst of the whole ordeal – worse even than the first clenching agony in his chest, the first tingling in his left hand, the hot narrowing certainty that it was actually happening. He was in that room, alone. Hospital hours have a sluggish, garbled rhythm. IV tubes slithered around the bedclothes whenever he moved his arm, and he felt both very intimate with and very remote from his own body – he was listening to it closely, waiting for the next thing, but it had failed him, nearly irrevocably, and he knew he would never be able to trust it again. He was bored, anxious, terrified, and lonely. He spent a long time daydreaming about a girlfriend from college, trying to remember what mattered to them, what they talked about for so many hours. He was reading an article in *Sports Illustrated* about the upcoming football season when he burst into tears. Upon her return, he told Beth none of this, but stared at her until she asked him what he wanted. All he could say was that he wanted to come home as soon as possible. What those solitary hours in the hospital recalled to him, more than anything else, was that he was grateful for the family that was his. Those hours concentrated the idea into a serum, individual drops running warmly down his throat. His life began in a broken family, a fucked-up family, and he had managed to build one that wasn't. He knew precisely how much that was worth.

Almost out of the room, he pauses and returns to the desk, where he picks up the card his brother dropped off, a ring of moisture in the middle from the glass. Carefully he reads it once more. Calling out, he asks his wife if she wants a drink. He can't make out the reply, which he assumes was no; Beth's never been much of a drinker. He'll ask again when he returns to her. Before going, he opens his fingers and drops the card straight into the trash can, where it floats, an island of white upon the dark, mute sea.

For Paul to have agreed to drink a beer with Pirro means that he truly does not want to walk home, which in itself is even more worrisome than the prospect now of manufacturing conversation with a man who is, it must be said, a stranger. The silence is amicable enough, however, as Pirro steers around the cafe with the mop, occasionally stopping to make some remark about what's on the radio, or to point out some aspect of the store's operation he considers idiotic.

'The manager – he's Lebanese – he is a nice guy, but he doesn't know shit about running a business. I don't know why they don't fire him. First we run out of the hazelnut beans, then we run out of the orange-cranberry scones. Some people, that's their favorite! They want to know why we don't have them anymore.'

From time to time Paul looks out the window, but he never

sees anyone, or at least no one who would concern him: just cars, young couples, old drunks wandering home from the corner bar.

'It's late, huh? You have to go?'

Paul says he doesn't have to go.

'Do you have a wife?'

'No. I'm divorced.'

'Divorce, an ugly thing,' says Pirro. 'But maybe not always. Marriage can be a burden.' He sets aside the mop and retrieves a second beer; as he crooks it open, Paul notices the ring on his finger for the first time.

'Where do you live?'

'Gravesend. My wife is there. She cleans rooms at a hotel in Manhattan. If I stay here long enough she will be asleep by the time I get home!' He laughs and drinks lustily from his beer.

Paul closes his eyes. Gravity seems to draw him deeper into the chair: a sense of comfort stretches across him like an extra skin. His earlier drowsiness returns as a pleasurable lethargy. He has a cold beer in his hand, there's nowhere he needs to go, and talking with Pirro demands nothing great of him. A few minutes pass. Pirro speaks.

'I am always surprised Americans make such good beer.' They are drinking Brooklyn Lager. 'I used to think it was only Europeans who understood it.'

Paul eyes him. 'Aren't you Muslim?'

'Muslim, yes! I am from Bosnia. You know your stuff. But don't act surprised, my friend. Muslims drink. They say one mustn't take alcohol because it harms the body, but when you know all the other ways there are to harm the body, it doesn't seem so important. Besides,' he says, lifting the bottle to his lips, 'it is just so fucking good.'

Laughing, Paul takes a drink of his own.

'In Germany,' says Pirro, coming closer to Paul, 'they have

a toast. When you touch your friend's glass, you say, "Prost." Then you lock eyes until each man takes a drink.'

Paul makes an expression of amusement.

'It brings luck, they say.'

In the present silence the woodpecker's clack of two bottlenecks is enough to split the air like a bell. He fixes Pirro's eyes in his own. Both men are slow to drink. An unexpected sensation falls through Paul, like the floor dropping away, as if a single taste of alcohol had the strength of a gallon. Pirro's eyes, small brown globes, hang suspended in his own, and for an uncomfortable instant the emotional traffic across the small space is much too heavy, much too dense.

Paul says, 'My father died today.' He meant yesterday, but it doesn't matter. 'He was alive for ninety-six years,' he adds absentmindedly. 'Doesn't that seem long enough to fit two lives?'

He isn't sure why he says this now; it causes Pirro to look away, embarrassed. He mutters something, an inaudible word, who knows. At last Paul coughs out a retraction: 'Don't worry. Forget I even mentioned it.' He waves his arm to dismiss the subject altogether. Pirro walks away and returns with a fresh beer for Paul, and he gratefully finishes the one in his hand. They listen to the news, which has moved on to sports. The Winter Olympics are underway in Italy; an American man took the gold in an Alpine skiing event. After that come the results from the cricket match between India and Pakistan.

Pirro, who has gone back to mopping, says, 'Did you leave your wife, or she left you?'

'In some ways, it was mutual.'

'What does that mean?'

'We both agreed to it.'

'But one of you must have wanted it more than the other?'

Paul shrugs. 'That's hard to say. Claire's so—'

'Claire is your wife's name?'

Nodding, he says no more. He feels a sudden, palpable reticence: Pirro shouldn't know too much about him; he shouldn't know of Claire. Paul can feel the alcohol patrolling his blood. His face is warm. Holding the bottle to his lips, he lets the beer slosh coolly across them, and a swallow fills his mouth. He should stop before he has too much. Tomorrow is the funeral. But by the time the thought reaches the deeper, more sensual part of his brain, it is simply soaked up: his lips seek more, and his hand brings the bottle to his mouth without his mind having to ask it. His thoughts are in a dangerous place for a man with a drink in his hand – he's thinking of his ex-wife. He's missing her, and even feels the stirrings of an erection.

Outside, a dog barks. Paul lets the bulb of desire dim; concentrating on Pirro and his dull march around the floor helps. He must be close to finishing. Pirro stops and reaches for his beer. He says, 'When I first came here, I knew no one. Surrounded by people I did not understand, who did not understand me. All alone in a strange land. I could trust no one but God.'

Paul hears the dog bark again.

Pirro asks, 'Do you believe in God?'

'No.'

Holding the mop like a flagpole, Pirro makes a knowing expression; it isn't quite a smile. It seems to say that he expected as much. He goes behind the counter and begins lobbing the uneaten pastries into a black garbage bag.

Paul read once of a 'god module,' a quirk in the human design that inclines people in the direction of religion. The idea appeals to Paul – God hasn't ever been *out there*; instead he originates *in here* – but long ago, after giving up on faith, he decided that his own god module was broken.

131

The intricacy of existence begs for a creator to explain it, but if there is a god, his only act was to manufacture this astonishing contraption, the universe, with all its tiny rules and hidden symmetries, before setting it in motion. Human beings, like grass or planets, are derivatives of that universe: flakes of incidental matter, complicated clay and nothing more. God isn't watching.

He finishes his beer. The last swallow is quite warm. Behind the counter, Pirro's elbows flap as he makes a fat knot out of the ends of the garbage bag, and then he looks at Paul and smiles, holding up the whole thing for him to see as if it is something he has hunted and killed.

7

Seeing the three girls, teenagers, in front of the funeral parlor, he recalls Bruegel's *Icarus*: the ploughman, his face turned away, easing the cart's dull weight downhill; the ship's sail billowing into a triumphant breast as it leaves the harbor. These girls don't care about the death behind the white curtains. They are unaware of their own ghostly contours in the window, where the glass has leached the color from their dresses. They don't see. Every day, after school, they wait on the same block for the same bus, and the funeral home means as much to them as a parking meter. Laughing, the girls lean out from the curb into the street as the bus arrives, its brakes wailing, its horn piping one abrupt warning. They jump back, just in time. The driver hardly notices as they board, still in giggles, and Paul watches the bus pull away before he goes inside.

The entrance greets him with practical smells, ammonia and potpourri, which he failed to notice on his first visit, when he was ushered along with such haste into the building's more modern offices. The wholesome decor in the front hall wants to suggest the house of a favorite grandmother — stately furniture, thick carpet. But that smell kills the effect. The aromas of cooking, of life, are missing. Wolff waits for him, wearing an expression that he has obviously refined over the years, a blend of geniality, pity, and professional distance. His suit is nicer than Paul's. The cuffs sit exactly where they ought to. The tie keeps its knot without complaint. Wolff's suit betrays no loose threads, no flatness of tone. Of course; he wears one every day.

Instead of shaking, Wolff claps a hand on Paul's shoulder, a rehearsed gesture of fraternity; the physical sensation jolts him. He has a mild hangover – after leaving Pirro last night he couldn't sleep and had a few more in the stuffy, embryonic darkness of his apartment, and he never drinks enough water anyway – which fades from one corner of his brain only to relight itself in another.

'Paul? It's time.'

In the rows of otherwise empty chairs sit two old men whose faces mean nothing to Paul. This comes as a surprise. They both wear rumpled brown suits, and one actually has a hat in his lap. He wonders briefly if a cult of funeral attendance exists among the elderly. It would serve as a kind of rehearsal, an enactment of that old wish: to witness one's own memorial and hear one's own eulogies, to see the women's tears. But, no, these must be men who knew his father. They turn: one flashes a mouthful of false teeth; the other closes his eyes and tucks his lips inward in an expression of condolence. They know he's the son. He should greet them now, thank them for coming, but he can't. Strangers would upset his mind's fragile silence. He quickly inserts himself in a seat at the front, and only then does he notice the urn that holds his father's ashes, elevated on a pedestal and pinned down by two beams of yellow light. It's simple, as requested. He asked for the most basic model on the market.

At the back of the room the door opens. Someone enters and then abruptly halts. The footsteps belong to a man, and before he turns Paul is certain who it is. This, too, comes as a surprise.

Ben takes a seat in the last row. The two old men dwell upon the sight of him, but neither says anything. They don't even smile. He's dressed in an impeccable suit and makes clear his disdain for the surroundings, disclosing it with a flicker of his eyes. He blinks in Paul's direction, as much of a greeting as he's willing to offer.

The minister enters, a man with a benevolent, unmemorable face, topped by a puff of white hair like meringue. He establishes himself at the lectern and clears his throat. Unitarian. He was hired at Wolff's late urging, in spite of Paul's insistence that religion be denied a place at the ceremony. But somebody had to speak, and Paul declined to perform the eulogy himself; he could not imagine finding words that expressed that difficult mixture of candor and fondness.

'I would like to begin with a psalm,' the minister says. The room is quiet as he finds his place. He starts: 'I lift up my eyes to the hills — from where will my help come?'

Because the idea of a silent vigil terrified him — it would have been absurd to sit and wait for the clock to shave off a certain number of minutes before he could stand, collect his father's ashes, and leave — Paul now sits compliantly and listens to a man of God recite from the Bible. He idly recalls the amount of money this sermon has cost him. But since others have come he's glad to have agreed to this one conventional chapter of a funeral. Like few other rites, funerals demand the upkeep of appearances, and even a man who does not believe in God can occasionally be grateful that the belief in God exists to shelter the most difficult moments. 'The sun shall not strike you by day, nor the moon by night.' He turns briefly to look at Ben, who this time does not return the glance, and who otherwise gives no sign of what inspired this change of heart. 'The Lord will keep you from all evil; he will keep your life.'

One of the old men plays with his rings, turning them around his fingers like dials.

The minister finishes: 'The Lord will keep your going out and your coming in from this time on and forevermore.'

He looks out at the four men in the audience, then says: 'Let us bow our heads and think of Frank, and of Frank's life.' Paul does so, and wonders if Ben does the same. The minister lifts his head and offers the lectern to anyone who wants to say a few words about the deceased, and one of the elderly men, leaning heavily on a cane, struggles up from his chair.

'I barely knew him,' the man begins, his speech halting and his eyes scrunched up behind heavy glasses, a case of extreme myopia. 'Frank's lived two floors above me for years. Can't even remember how long it's been anymore. And I never heard a peep out of him until maybe six or seven years ago, when I was laid up after back surgery. Couldn't move a muscle. A nurse came two hours every day, but she was no good, she didn't give a damn about me. Frank said he'd pick up the newspaper and some groceries for me every morning. Frank had his own health problems – it wasn't easy for him to get around, either. He offered. I never asked him to do it. For a year he brought me the newspaper. Otherwise, I can tell you, I'd of gone mad in that apartment by myself. Keeping up to date on what the president was saying, on the craziness in the world, made me feel like I was still a human being, like my seat was still saved. If not for Frank I'd of lost every marble.'

The man steps down from the lectern, his hands shaking, and returns to his seat. No one else volunteers to speak. The minister returns to the dais and, after loudly clearing his throat, opens to another psalm.

Ben is still there at the end of the ceremony, his posture a bit sunken but firm, the suit across his shoulders as hard as pavement. Paul half expected his brother to have slipped out partway through, once he'd proved his point, whatever that was. His eyes are closed and his head is bowed. He looks as stony and distant as a figure in a photograph. Paul is about to say hello before realizing what is happening. He steps back and waits for his brother to finish praying.

A hand catches his elbow. It's the man who spoke. He leans on his cane, his back bent into the curve of a scythe, his body shrunken like a leaf of paper curled in the fire; his eyes have withered to slits. Paul wonders how he moves around without constantly crashing into the furniture.

'You're Frank's son.'

'Paul.'

'He was a good man, your father.'

'I appreciate that. Not many people would get up there and say what you did.'

'About Frank? Quietest man I ever knew. Not a mean bone in his body.'

He shoves out his hand and Paul takes it, surprised by the firmness of the grip.

'Shel Greenberg.'

'Mr Greenberg — it's a pleasure to meet you. I'm sure my father would have been glad to know you were here.'

Paul fits himself into the passenger's seat of Ben's car. In the backseat, propped in the corner, is the urn; Wolff assured him that the lid was fastened tightly and wouldn't come off, even if it fell over. Ben's eyes hold the road ahead in a fixed stare, and he doesn't speak, just as he hasn't spoken since they left the funeral parlor. He drives with one arm, extended perfectly straight like a running back's. They merge with traffic onto the Williamsburg Bridge. It isn't yet six; at Ben's suggestion they are going to have dinner. The first meal the brothers will have shared in years.

'Thank you,' says Paul. 'For coming.' He hopes to prompt Ben into an explanation, but Ben offers none, nothing at all, and the brothers sit in silence the rest of the way.

Ben takes them to an Italian restaurant on the Upper West Side. He seems to know the maître d', who seats them at a table in a back corner, away from the general drift of early-evening diners; only the candles on each table interrupt the crepuscular mood of the room, sunken below street level, walls the color of eggplant. Ben orders a bottle of red wine while Paul absentmindedly glances at the menu. He asks for the first thing his eyes settle on. His attention returns to his brother – his stern, mute brother, whose face the candle-light holds in a severe shadow. The candle's own shadow creates a shivering meniscus on the wall.

'If I'd known you were going to have that,' says Ben, 'I'd have told you to get something else. The calamari here is good.'

Paul nods. If all Ben has in mind is criticizing his dining habits, they can eat in silence.

'Beth says you stopped by the apartment.'

'Just to leave the card. I tried calling first. You didn't answer.' Paul takes a sip of water. After a long pause, he says, 'You haven't been in the same room with Dad for decades.'

'I wasn't going to come,' his brother says quickly. 'I haven't forgiven Frank, and I won't, ever. That's not why I came.'

The waiter returns with the wine. Ben swallows the first taste and nods tersely. The glasses are poured, the waiter leaves. Neither man speaks. Ben pinches the neck of the bottle between thumb and forefinger and rotates it so that he can read the writing on the back of the label.

He says, 'My wife thought it was a good idea. She thought it would give me closure.'

Ben is not a man who casually uses terms like 'closure.' He speaks the word with a certain halting pronunciation.

'In Judaism, the laws of mourning apply to the father's son,' he adds. 'No matter who the father was.'

'I saw you praying.'

'That wasn't for him.'

Ben takes an intemperate drink from his wineglass.

Paul says, 'You wouldn't have been wrong to pray for him, you know. He was an old man. He suffered.'

'That man got ninety-six years of life,' says Ben, his voice softening. 'Ninety-six years. More than most. More than almost all. That man got the lion's share of life.'

In poor light his face has the firmness of granite. Time for Ben has not mollified his hatred or made it a fossil: it remains a living, changing part of his inner geology, growing, deepening, hardening. Whatever his reasons for coming to the funeral, they do not include a wish for a posthumous rapprochement with their father.

'Prayer just seems unlike you,' says Paul.

'Of course I pray,' snaps Ben. 'I'm a Jew. I pray.'

At the time, Ben's conversion seemed no more than a blunt renunciation of the name Metzger. Paul always assumed that his brother's enthusiasm for the endeavor was a secular one, a family affair, and had nothing to do with holding God in esteem.

'I just never thought you had that kind of weakness.'

'Weakness?' Ben snorts as he takes another drink. 'Faith in God is a weakness? Then why is it such a struggle? Believing, continuing to believe in the face of the shit life throws at you requires strength.'

He drinks again.

'You, for one, couldn't believe in God.'

Paul drinks from his wine. He says, 'Maybe it does take strength to believe in God, but it takes just as much to forgive a bad father his mistakes.'

'This has nothing to do with being a bad father.'

'That's because he wasn't a bad father to you. He loved you. You're the son he wanted.' He drinks; the wine tastes dense and earthy. 'What better proof than that he waited so long to take you out of the will?'

Seemingly indifferent to Paul's words, Ben takes a piece of bread from the basket and tears it apart. 'I spoke to my lawyer again,' he says, chewing. 'And, for the record, Frank was a lousy father to me, too.'

'But you still insist on taking his money.'

'I've explained this to you. I've got no intention of keeping the damned money. It isn't his to have, or to give – it's got to be taken from him.'

'Bullshit, Ben. That's bullshit. All this about – about what, exactly? Reparations? Extracted from the estate of Frank Metzger, by you, on behalf of the Jewish people?'

'Whether you believe me or not is irrelevant. You're the second-born.'

'Then you're the never-born! The only reason he waited so long to take you out of the will was that he kept hoping you'd come back. He kept hoping you'd forgive him.'

'I wasn't ever going to forgive him. He understood that. He knew that, at least.'

'You talk about believing in God, and here you are, robbing a dead man.'

'The point here is you, Paul. You want the little money Frank managed not to squander in your bank account.'

'I'm thirty-six years old and I'm broke. Of course I want it. Look at you – you manage a hedge fund. You fucking print money for a living.'

'I've told you, I'm not *keeping* his goddamned money. This

has nothing to do with money. If you want me to give you a loan, I'll do it.'

'Would you even be able to, in the current climate?' Paul, on the verge of saying more, restrains himself. 'This isn't the point.'

'No, it isn't.'

'You left. I stayed behind. I stayed his son. Hate me for that if you want, but the fact is that when he died he had only one living heir.'

'You've already been to a lawyer, haven't you? What did he tell you? I know what he told you — that you can't beat this in court. Anybody's going to tell you that.'

'I'm not taking you to court.'

'I know you aren't.' He pauses. Paul sees a mouthful of purplish wine-stained teeth. 'We're family.'

The waiter again. He lowers two steaming plates onto the table before vanishing. Paul has already forgotten what he ordered: an oily spaghetti glistens under a stew of tomatoes, zucchini, and what looks like sausage. He winds a few strands around his fork. It tastes fine, a little salty, but as he chews, it becomes flavorless and rubbery between his teeth, heavy on the tongue; he swallows quickly. Ben doesn't eat, only stabs at the corners of his mouth with his napkin. Staring at Paul, he lifts his knife, then sets it down. His fingers, not his face, disclose his agitation: he rubs them together as if testing a banknote.

He says, 'Nothing I can say is going to make you understand. I would maybe keep trying if I thought there was any chance.'

'You are the most bullheaded son of a bitch I know,' says Paul. 'That's why I was surprised to find you praying. Of all people, you seem least in need of outside approval. You make up your mind and will listen to no other argument. Not even one that comes directly from God.'

'Is that who I am?'

As he says this, Ben looks weary. Many fail where Ben succeeded – pulling himself apart from the identity handed to him at birth, no matter what the cost. Men have always tried to tear off the skin of family, the weight, to be greater than what they were given, to be better and sturdier and wiser, to be more important. They almost always fail. Ben has been tireless in scrubbing away the dead history. Paul always assumed it came easily to him, as naturally as breathing, but now he realizes the truth: his brother's has been a life of work. The man sitting on the other side of the table is a creation entirely of his own design.

He says, 'I got an offer to do a book.'

'Yeah.' Relief floods Ben's face; he, too, wants a reprieve. 'You mentioned something about it – the cartoons, right? Those riots? You know, it occurred to me the other day, your book, and I think it's terrific. Someone needs to write about it. There's too much apology going on, too much coddling of these fanatics. All this lip service paid to tolerance. We're just supposed to tolerate murder and lunacy? In my opinion, it's just another kind of terrorism. It's insane, all those people running around, yelling about the desecration of their prophet, all because of a few stupid cartoons. How many embassies have they destroyed? Christ. It makes you think that the world is going to end, that they're really going to blow it all up.'

Paul waits for his brother to finish, then shakes his head. He says, 'I'm going to write a book about Dad.'

Ben sets down his glass.

'It's going to be a memoir. Sort of. An editor is—'

His brother cuts him off. 'Frank? About Frank?'

'Ben, listen—'

'You're going to preserve that man in print?'

It jars him, always, the velocity with which Ben can swerve

into hostility. He doesn't give Paul a chance to elaborate, to clarify. Ben has drummed against that soreness which stretches across any thought of their father, and it causes a sudden, acute ire to materialize within him – his chest feels like a set of tightly clamped teeth – and so, instead of explaining his plans for the book, he finds himself, once more, annotating the father for the sake of the brother.

'That man who spoke,' says Paul, his voice rising a little, 'that man who got up and talked about Dad? You remember. His name was Greenberg. Shel Greenberg. He said that for a full year Dad got him newspapers and groceries, and his name was fucking *Greenberg*. Dad must've known that. If he carried around such hatred in his heart, if he was such a bigot, how did he bring himself to perform this act of kindness, day in and day out, an entire year of favors, for a Jew?'

'You're saying that buying the *Daily News* and a few melons for some softheaded old retiree makes up for what he did? You're saying that a year of small chores in the service of a neighbor is all it takes? That anyone can be absolved of his crimes by the testimony of a few neighbors? Let's go down to Argentina then. I'm sure Eichmann's neighbors adored him. I'll bet they were truly saddened when Mossad kicked in the door and hauled him off. The conversation was probably the same for days afterward: "He was such a nice man, loved his daughters."'

'Eichmann had sons, actually.'

'I don't care! Frank can buy newspapers for thirty Greenbergs. I don't care.' Ben grasps at his glass of wine and a mouthful churns up to his lips. 'He can take them all out for matzo-ball soup. I don't care.'

'This man cared. Shel Greenberg cared. He didn't even have to convert to make his point.'

This has the desired effect. Ben drinks sourly from his glass.

Paul says, 'You can refuse to forgive Dad, if that's what you want. But he was a human being. He was as complicated and fucked up as anyone else. It isn't all a matter of good and evil.'

Ben sighs. He drags the fork across the tablecloth like a plow, leaving four parallel striations that quickly fade.

'He swore his allegiance to Hitler. Frank wasn't a child. He wasn't coerced. You do that and it's over. You're done. There is no coming back from that kind of moral ruin. Was Hitler "complicated"? Just fucked up? Tell me, Paul. Tell me what, since you refuse to believe in evil.'

'Our father wasn't Hitler.'

'Isn't it a luxury, this reasonableness of yours.'

'Shut up, Ben. I'm just trying to be calm.'

'Fine, be calm. You fucking be the calm one. I apologize that in the face of what my father did I don't have the ability to remain calm. I'm sick of this. I'm sick of trying to explain to you what should be plainly fucking obvious. At this point it's your willful ignorance as much as anything that pisses me off. That you think you're only being a good son, or whatever.'

They fall into silence. Ben chews heatedly on a bite of food. He speaks of Paul's choices — his faithlessness, his unwillingness to discard their father — as signs of weakness, as if they somehow represent a failure of manhood, and Paul, in response, feels a rare anger, the kind that licenses rashness, surrounding otherwise stupid actions with something like glee. He stares at his brother, whose eyes seem indissolubly dark, pupil and iris melting into a single inkblot.

'What would you do if God told you to?'

'Excuse me?'

'You're willing to condemn the protestors who say they're defending their prophet, but you believe, too. You speak so vehemently of it, your belief. Tell me what you would do.'

'Are you trying to lump me in with those nuts?'

'Why not?'

'Christ, Paul.'

'Terrorists believe in God, too. Even more fully than you.'

'Fuck you, if you want to talk like that.'

The words tremble below his tongue. 'What if God told you to blow yourself up?'

'Fuck you.' Ben wrestles his napkin from his lap and throws it into his uneaten food.

'What if God came down and tapped you on the shoulder. Then what? You pray, Ben, you believe in God. You say it takes such strength. It takes strength to fly planes into buildings, too.'

His brother signals to the waiter, who comes promptly, and before he can produce the check Ben shoves a credit card at him.

Paul says, 'Abraham would have slit his son's throat.' He feels light, elated. How easy this is, how perilously and thrillingly easy, to push and pull his brother's emotional levers. 'What if God told Abraham instead to strap a bomb to his chest, to fill his pockets with nails and ball bearings and broken glass, to board a bus at noon and detonate himself in the middle of a crowd of old ladies and little schoolchildren?'

'You've lost it, Paul. I don't hear a word of what you're saying. You're absolutely gone.'

'Do you defy God or do you kill innocent people? Did the terrorists simply choose the wrong god? Is that what you tell yourself?'

The waiter returns. Ben signs the form absently, leaves a large tip. He stands and rips his jacket off the back of the chair.

'What do you tell yourself, Ben? How does Ben Metzger make himself believe in God?'

Ben takes two steps away before stopping: something he's remembered. He turns and fixes Paul with his eyes.

'Come get your fucking father out of my car.'

Rain catches him between the subway and his apartment. He manages to protect the urn, holding it under his jacket, but the distance to his door is too great to spare himself a soaking. He doesn't immediately strip off his wet clothes. Instead, after setting the urn on the windowsill, the first available spot, he goes straight to the kitchen and retrieves a bottle of beer, then sits down on his wet bottom and watches the window, listening to the rain's soft, depressing applause. A car makes its way down the block, traveling at low speed, its headlights set to bright. It reaches the end of the block and idles. The malty scent of beer rises from the bottle's neck. Outside, the car seems to have found its way: it inches past the stop line, then gains speed and travels up the block into soupy darkness, out of view. The bottle is quickly gone. He retrieves another, and, after that, a third. Each bottle he finishes he sets on the floor, and they collect around his feet like a detachment of exhausted soldiers. He loses the grip on his anxiety, not from conscious effort, but because it has withered and become desiccated in the desert of his inebriation; the more he drinks, the drier he is, as the moisture leaves his lips, his tongue, his inward provinces.

His hand reaches for the phone and dials Claire's number. She will know he's drinking; he doesn't care. It rings several times before he hangs up. He tells himself once more that Sunday night, the memory of which has drifted and fractured already, did not for Claire represent the beginnings of a reunion. He doesn't know what she wanted. He knows only that it was different from what he wanted. Paul has another beer, then stands, waggling his arms and legs to start the blood moving. But even one step seems to upset some fragile, important balance. Paul hesitates, loses his footing. He's at the first stage of drunkenness, a little hazy, eager for more: eager to plunge his head underneath, into the congenial abyss that he knows awaits him on the other side of seven, eight, ten bottles. Morning will come, with its unwelcome renewal of sobriety, but in the meantime he can drink as much as he likes. Nobody's here to tell him otherwise. No funerals tomorrow, no meetings. He takes a step back, stumbles, kicks the bottles on the floor. They scatter in a babble of glass. It dies quickly; they settle on their sides. Silence is always most silent in the wake of a disturbance.

Enough. Deeply and suddenly tired, he removes his funeral clothes, his shoes, jacket, and tie, and makes a damp pile on the floor. Off, socks. Off, lights. He's already crawling onto the pullout as he tears away his shirt. Pants. In a quick motion, a wing beating once against the air, he plucks a tissue from the box on the nearby table. Claire forms. Images from Sunday night mix with older recollections. He's half erect as he begins, half erect as he finishes. With a tired shudder he comes into the tissue — hard to believe that this, under different circumstances, could father a child. He tosses it away, and for an instant it glides along the air, with the indifference of a dandelion puff, before sailing into the garbage.

He thinks again of Claire. His father. Ben. They are all too little, and, somehow, too much. Terence: a broken figure at the end of the street, cigarette jutting alertly from his lips. Abraham and Isaac, remembered from a painting he once saw: Isaac, blindfolded, his bare neck bulging with blood, and bald, bearded Abraham. His eyes are small, dark, and certain. The knife hangs like a raindrop frozen in midflight. The paint tells its age; Abraham's cheek splits apart like clay.

White wings, in the distance, descend upon petrified air. *Abraham, Abraham. Here I am.* As his mind sifts through these last vestiges of thought, as exhaustion rises into sleep, Paul finds it impossible to say which are worse, the angels who make themselves known to us, or the ones that never do.

8

He wakes to the sound of the telephone. It featured briefly in his dream, but he doesn't remember the form it took — bomb, doorbell, alarm. Nor can he recall what sort of dream it was, though he has the impression that it was vivid. The logic of nearby objects leads him back to the world. He reviews the proof of his identity: the wallet on the shelf, the clothes on the floor, the particular arrangement of chair, table, mirror. Nothing is distinct, lovingly or specially chosen. They are the things that belong to any man who lives alone. At the horizon of his thoughts throbs a vague but familiar sadness.

But it isn't his phone — the sound leaks in through the thin wall that separates his apartment from the neighbor's. At last it stops. He clears his eyes and looks out the window at the angled slab of sky, sawed off by the roofline of nearby buildings, the squat aluminum chimneys and abandoned television aerials. The view is newly obstructed: his father's urn hunches there, its blocky contours gracelessly slicing away a piece of scenery. Outside, the world is gray, not only failing to provide light but draining it from the room. A dead leaf, sailing on the wind, flickers briefly into view. He listens to the faint sizzle of morning traffic. Other people are awake.

As for Paul, he has awoken into the familiar, constricted pain of a hangover: his tongue feels monstrous and blistery;

his bladder is pinched; sweat grips his face all the way down to his neck. He needs to drink less, and less often. He looks again at the urn and an impulse strikes him. He rises, shaves, showers. He bolts a large glass of water. After drying and dressing, he collects the urn from the sill and leaves.

He goes to the lake in the park. The peppery, whitish ash, which he expected to dissolve like powdered lemonade, clumps and drifts like algae on the surface of the cold water; he waits for it to sink and afterward deposits the empty urn in the first trash can he passes. He feels a shudder as it drops, as it hits bottom, thudding with the strength of something full. This improvisation must violate the laws of burial – the religious ones, surely, and perhaps even the civil ones; human remains may even constitute a health hazard. And certainly he has already disobeyed some rule of mourning: he has almost certainly disobeyed all of them. Not knowing what else to do with himself, he walks to the cafe, where he sees Pirro, pinballing from cash register to espresso machine and back, busily conveying cups between the two. There's a line. It is a Friday and people have given themselves permission to go into work a little late. Reaching under the counter, Pirro brings up a pair of fat morning muffins, their surfaces knobby with bright red berries, and deftly wraps them in purses of wax paper. He won't have a chance to talk, which is a relief, actually. He smiles at Paul, who has reached the front of the line. 'Cold today,' he says. 'But they say the sun comes back tomorrow.'

'If that's what they say.'

'Thank God.'

'Small coffee.'

He pays and turns to go. He has a vague awareness that he should say something more, to acknowledge that he and Pirro are now more than the transaction between customer and server; but they aren't, and he can't. Instead he calls

Claire. Her voice appears abruptly on the fourth ring, after she has seen his name on her phone's screen and, he can be sure, deliberated before answering; until now he's forgotten that he called her last night as well.

He says, 'He's dead.'

She needs a second to interpret this. 'Your father?'

'Yes. Tuesday.'

'How are you?'

He makes no reply. His ear fills with Claire's impatient breathing.

'Can I see you?'

The line falls silent. 'When?'

'Now.'

'I have to go to work.'

'Just for a little while. Please, Claire.' He hates the plaintive note that creeps into his voice.

She pauses long enough that he thinks the signal may have been lost. At last she says: 'Okay. I can go in a little late today. But hurry up.' He tries to ignore the suggestion, in her tone, that she owes him this, that she hasn't agreed to see him so much as to give him an audience.

Manhattan. He changes lines. The train he boards is crowded enough that there is nowhere to sit. He always wonders about these people, who, like him, are not at work during work hours. Everyone has a reason. His profession is respectable enough, and he doesn't hang his head when someone asks what he does — he does not have to say he is unemployed — but he nonetheless feels an associated discomfort at being part of this slack daylight tribe. The inertia of these lives is palpable. Heads toss gently from side to side like drowsy underwater reeds as the train makes a ramshackle approach into the flooding lights of the Astor Place station. He feels calmer now, closer to Claire; only a handful of stops remain. Paul has no idea what he plans to say.

He isn't proud of using his father's death as a crowbar to break into his wife's day, but the thought of seeing her makes him happy in a simple way, although he knows he shouldn't let himself have such naive emotions. What is he expecting? To sleep with her again? No, he tells himself, I am not expecting that. I just want to see her and speak with her. Paul studies the passengers around him, their bodies fattened by winter layers: closed eyes, numb staring eyes, collapsed shoulders, heads sinking into open pages. People do read, then, at least on the subway. He sees tabloid newspapers, miniature Bibles, self-help guides with titles like *Growing Through Divorce* and *The Science of Getting Rich* and *Healing Back Pain*. Then, at the end of the car, he spots a face which, like an actor's from a half-remembered film, is familiar without at once being identifiable, and the agitation opens slowly within him, delicately unwrapping itself. Terence must have been following him all morning.

They come to another station. Paul stands at one set of doors, and as passengers board and depart, bumping and prodding him, he keeps his eyes pinned on Terence, who does not return his gaze, as if he's just another commuter, an innocent platelet in the midday flow. The heat of the platform feels as close as breath from a mouth on Paul's neck, and under his coat, under his shirt, perspiration springs up, forming a thick glaze; uncontrollable processes — in his heart and his veins, in his lungs — fire up throughout his body. The train pulls out of the station.

It moves with the lazy cow's waddle that means it closely follows the train ahead. The next stop is Claire's. When Paul looks again, Terence has vanished. His eyes search wildly and he picks him up, that cap of pale hair, moving toward him through the car. He tenses. But Terence stops, lowering himself into a seat that has opened up, one from which he has a direct line of sight to Paul. They watch each other through the thicket of limbs, heads, torsos, until Terence glances away. It is oddly chilling.

He has to make a plan. Terence can't do much here, in a train car packed with human insulation, but if there has to be some sort of confrontation, if the particles of hostility that hang about him assemble into violence, it cannot happen at Claire's doorstep. Paul could pretend that he's not about to disembark and then slip between the doors: Terence might miss it. Paul tightens his grip around the handlebar as the train slows. The moment has a terrible surface tension. He balances on the balls of his feet and, out of the corner of his eye, observes Terence, who sits alertly. A mechanical whisper indicates that the doors are about to open: he leans toward them and for an instant separates his gaze from his pursuer. The doors open. Before moving he looks once to check on Terence and finds that he has gotten to his feet, his eyes fixed firmly and attentively upon Paul — those eyes, brown and even a little sullen, as if wounded that he would even consider sneaking off. The doors shut and they are once again on their way.

Terence looks away again, almost with a shrug, as soon as the train is out of the station. They have been at this little game long enough that Paul's initial fear has dulled and, as his chance to see Claire passes, it cools into annoyance. Terence wants to see what he can get away with, how long Paul will put up with him. Still, a face-off, even in the safety of a public place, seems unwise. Paul needs to put distance between them. Later, he will have to phone the police again, and this time he must make them take his complaint seriously; he will go down to the station, give a description, explain the pattern of harassment. For now, he can get off in midtown and use the size and drift of crowds to his advantage. The train clocks through two more stations; Terence stands in wait as serenely as a mannequin.

Grand Central comes and goes with a great respiratory exchange of passengers, and, at Fifty-first Street, Paul makes his move. Without even looking – surely he is being followed – he slingshots through the doors and pushes toward the front of the crowd as it slows and branches into thin capillaries at the gates. Enough people become like water; they force an exit. Someone punches through the emergency gate, igniting the alarm's dizzy ululation. Paul slips through the scarred iron door – for him this qualifies as an emergency – and once more he emerges at street level.

Rainwater stands at the curb in silver puddles, and a high, stern sun glares down. Paul extends his strides as he turns east. He passes through the warm, chalky steam blossoming from the vents of a laundromat, through the salt-and-lard odor at the door of a Chinese takeaway joint, through the bent shadows of fire escapes and empty stoops. The light at Third Avenue halts him and he turns south. Unaccustomed to exercise and already starved for oxygen, the muscles in his legs burn and complain, cramping into aching little knots, and Paul curses under his breath, furious at his body's unreliability, furious at himself for failing to halt its decline. What is he afraid of? What can Terence do to him out in the open? He crosses Third Avenue at Forty-ninth Street, jogging to beat the serrated edge of advancing cars; the nasal snort of a horn admonishes him just as he hops onto the next curb. He wants to lose Terence in the lunchtime crowds near the river. Tourists clot in front of a man selling cheap neckties and belts, and Paul wades through them.

Turning onto Forty-eighth Street, he nearly collides with someone, and when he looks up to apologize he recognizes the face. The man is an actor, a relatively famous one, and he is eating an apple; his lips are bright with juice. Startled,

Paul walks past, and he now sees that he has stumbled upon the set of a film. Men with headsets wave to each other and write on clipboards, and others march in and out of long white trucks. On the sidewalk is a table littered with food: bagels, muffins, sliced fruit, a steel urn of coffee. White screens, stretched like sails, frame the entrance to an apartment building in the middle of the block, along with equally large mirrors, angled expectantly upward; lamps the size of car tires splash everything in unnatural white light. He doesn't see any cameras.

He emerges onto Second Avenue, continuing south, and can find no sign of Terence, although that doesn't mean anything. He crosses the avenue toward Hammarskjöld Plaza and only when he is halfway between sidewalks does he notice the gathering on the opposite side of the street. Crowds he was expecting, but these people are collected in the hundreds — they number perhaps more than a thousand — and they clearly belong together; they have the slack knitting of an audience at a concert. Paul then sees that their attention is directed at a man standing in front of a microphone and dressed from head to toe in white.

He mixes into the group's raggedy fringe. Here and there stand uniformed police officers, laden with metal and gear, and on a rooftop high above he sees the glint from a pair of binoculars. A television crew hangs off to the side. Above the belt of the river, flags, certain of their importance, straighten in the wind. Terence has disappeared. Paul presses deeper into the crowd, and eventually finds himself in its concentrated heart, where he can barely move. Most of the faces around him aren't white.

The man addressing the crowd has been speaking in a language Paul doesn't recognize, but suddenly he switches to English. 'The burning of buildings and the loss of lives have been unacceptable. People who love God and Muhammad are becoming overwhelmed by their anger.' He goes on. It's about the cartoons, then – this, too, is a protest, like those he has seen on television, with their scorched flags and burning cars and vandalized embassies. Applause crackles around Paul. The strange weather that ripples through those crowds overseas doesn't seem to have taken hold here: people are attentive and calm; a policeman checks his wristwatch as the speaker slips again into what must be Arabic. Men in black flank him, in stark contrast to his white robes; behind sunglasses they wear stoic expressions. Security men.

The speech continues. Growing concerned about his lack of mobility, Paul begins to thread his way to the other side, toward the horizon of the East River and the rough face of Queens, where the Citigroup tower stands awkwardly upon the low borough. He is aided by a loosening of the crowd, for which he detects no apparent cause; people are pulling apart, creating channels of space. He checks again for Terence. As he reaches the other edge, he notices the movement around him. They're turning as one to face the river – and, because it is where he happens to be, Paul. Has he done something? But their eyes all gaze beyond him, well beyond him, beyond the river and Queens, beyond even the Atlantic Ocean. He recognizes at once what this is. A voice of warm monotony, with a cello's plangent timbre, puffs out across the clumps of heads, intoning words Paul doesn't know. The call to prayer. It is followed by silence. For the space of a breath nothing happens, and then, at once, the hundreds of bodies fall, like blades of grass blown flat by the wind; the sound rolls over him like the sound from a building collapsing in the distance. They are humble, devout, good. People fold their legs and prostrate themselves, hands clapped to the concrete, foreheads balanced between them like delicate ceramics; they use sliced-up cardboard boxes and unfurled garbage bags to protect their knees from the damp ground. Paul's head pounds. He has never seen so many people pray at once: it is like seeing a tidal wave for the first time, or a tornado, an asteroid. He was part of this crowd a moment ago, one of many, and now he stands alone; now, even worse, he is in the way.

Small birds, winter scavengers, twist above the river. His coat whips around jauntily; the wind gains strength and the fragile puddles nearby respond with ecstatic little vibrations. Clouds converge on the sun and around him the light melts away. He is cold and slightly shaking, and he wants to get out of the aim of their prayer. He looks up and around at the high, imperious faces of office buildings. This particular block is secluded in its madness: the man chasing him, the demonstration, the massive collective prayer. The rest of the city is right now like the people in these buildings, locked away in dry aquariums behind clean glass surfaces. There is another pause in the imam's speech. The congregation rises as suddenly as it fell. The entire episode has a frequency to which all but Paul are attuned, a pious choreography. More words follow; but this chapter of speech is brief, and once again they fall with spectacular calm.

He starts to move away. A hiccup in the concrete snags his shoe and he stumbles, as if missing a square in hopscotch. Paul looks up. It feels like an agnostic insult, this startled jerky motion he has made, but they are concentrating on God, not him. No one gives any sign of noticing – no one except the solitary figure on the opposite side of the crowd. He stands there, watching Paul, and smiles faintly.

Once more the crowd rises; Terence disappears behind it. Paul doesn't wait. He makes a hard diagonal across the plaza, back toward Second Avenue, where he presses into the flow of people, close quarters that lock him into a fast walk. Paul fights against the tidal push of the avenue. Gone are the calm, contemplative expressions of people at prayer; wherever he looks now, the faces are proud, preoccupied, shatterproof. Dozens of bodies occupy a single frame of vision, some paused, some in motion, some alone, some in groups: metropolitan density is too much for the human eyeball to sort. A single block of New York City is an immense concentration of detail and circumstance, and Paul's brain, like his muscles, isn't trained to work in this reactive mode. A quick surveillance finds no sign of Terence, which means he either fell behind or has concealed himself once again. Paul walks north, looking up the narrowing avenue to where it finally vanishes altogether.

Fresh crowds pack the sidewalk. In the distance he can still hear the speaker, his words like the solitary tolling of a church bell on the other side of a hill. Paul turns around, then turns again. Up and down the avenue – in doorways, under awnings, behind piles of garbage – Terence is nowhere to be seen. Coats flap in the wind. A plastic bag scuttles through legs and feet like a crab.

He waits. Nothing happens. He walks back to the subway in a blind daze, looking around once or twice. It is almost one o'clock, which means that Claire left for work long ago.

In the station he jostles a round woman loaded down with shopping bags, who shoots him a dirty look. He doesn't care. A train must have just left: there is no one else waiting. Paul walks to the end of the platform, past the last bench, and stands by a black, sulking garbage can. In his peripheral vision he is aware of the platform filling. He finally hears the train and senses that first slipping of the station's air. At last there's a light. The tracks begin to glow. Air piles against the side of Paul's face as the train hurtles into the station. The doors open, he enters, and they close again with a sigh. He takes a grip of the handlebar and closes his eyes, exhausted. On his back the cool sweat starts to dry.

But the train doesn't move. Seconds accumulate. Paul opens his eyes and immediately sees the reason. Three fingers with rough, pitted nails have stuck themselves in the door, between the lips of black rubber, and on the other side Terence hovers like a figure in a nightmare.

The doors stutter; Paul holds his breath. They are inches apart, separated only by the sheath of bad glass in the door: in the pressure chamber of their silent exchange the seconds slow: they do not move. The fineness of Terence's face surprises him, as white as the inside of a halved apple; with the pale hair it burns glossily against the scum and spit of the station wall, the dun, bony tiles. At his throat, under the black leather jacket, is a triangle of yellowish white. His eyes make terse, tiny adjustments: they are assessing Paul, gathering and storing information. A hard bulge distends the skin under his ear and throbs like a baby heart — he's chewing gum. Paul takes a step back as a shudder runs through the metal doors. He considers making an effort to pry out the fingers, but Terence spares him the trouble. He snatches away his hand; the doors proudly snap shut. At last the train pulls away, but Paul can't take his eyes from Terence, whose lips are peeled back from his teeth in a grin.

The forest of champagne flutes on the long white table, occupying an entire side of the museum's main hall, makes Claire think of all the ways they could shatter. Members of the catering staff, clothed in starched black shirts, flock and flow nearby as they make the last preparations, gathering heaps of ice in metal buckets and setting out soldierly rows of bottles. Tonight the museum hosts the reception for the mounting of its newest acquisition. Belonging to an after-hours crowd gives Claire an enjoyable, almost mischievous feeling, like those evenings as a teenager when for one reason or another she found herself back inside her high school. Buildings have distinct personalities, connected to their purposes and hours of use, and to inhabit one at an off-time — to denude the museum of its serious attire and fill it with liquor and the insistent roar of a dinner party — stirs up the exhilaration of trespass. Perhaps this is enough to account for her peculiar mood, her speculation about the ways the night could fail, beginning with the destruction of a thousand glasses of good champagne. The most spectacular version she can devise involves the highly improbable toppling of the twenty-four-foot sculpture in steel that looms darkly in the center of the atrium.

The guests have yet to arrive. In the past months Claire has been a quick study, memorizing the identity and importance of hundreds of people whose capital animates the ecosystem of the New York art world. Working in galleries, she came into contact with many of their ilk, but it's an entirely different tribe that inhabits the rarefied atmosphere of museum endowment. And they will, very many of them, be here tonight. As planned, *Century* now hangs in its new home, the south wall of the atrium, framed by an enormous white expanse. A short article ran today in the Arts section of the *Times*; everyone was thrilled. Later, Bernard will make a brief toast, less in celebration of the art than as a testament to the donors who made its purchase possible; he will stress the lasting value of their investment, the pride of place that *Century* will hold in the museum's permanent collection when, after its tenure in the atrium, it's moved to the fourth floor among the other postwar giants.

Paul's failure to appear this morning distracts her only a little. Sunday night is already abstract and distant, an historical event; today she waited at the apartment as long as she could. Frankly, she was relieved when he didn't come, as cruel as that makes her feel.

Someone squeezes her arm from behind. The sensation is sudden and unwelcome, and it immediately sets her on edge, but she relaxes upon turning to find Bernard's pink old face, its wispy white hair and soft patrician jowl. For a man of his importance and longevity, he's surprisingly easy to be around, his attention always safely avuncular. Others cluck at his habit of tediously expatiating, in his light British accent, one of education and casual privilege, on this or that matter — and at his ability to bring any subject around to himself, the grand narrative of his first-rate life. He's met everyone, seen everything, been everywhere. Just the same, Claire is fond of Bernard and, at his better moments, finds him fiercely charming.

'Have you girded yourself for the advancing army, my dear?'

She smiles, waits for him to go on.

'Each of them will take the usual three minutes to stare at the painting and then wander off, glass of champagne in hand — my God, you would think they hadn't ever had champagne before, the way they slurp it up! Then off to find the plaques in the museum that hold their names. Or, in the case of many, their mothers' names.'

At six they appear. Bernard brings around one or two notables and makes the introductions. Claire has a glass of champagne, surprised by how quickly it takes her; champagne, more than any other drink, gives her a wonderful lightness, like compressed air under the soles of her feet. New faces appear by the minute. David's isn't one of them. She will do fine with or without him, even if it must be said that he has a talent for this sort of event, the sport of socializing; she always feels somewhat ill at ease in this company, somewhat unlike herself. Champagne helps. She shouldn't have much more: the party technically counts as work. The men climbing the stairs from the lobby all seem to be much older, and reliably they have younger wives on equivalent arms. The women of their age who come are often widows. She and David have spoken once since Wednesday, by phone – a short, almost businesslike conversation; he hasn't stopped by her office.

Discreetly, Claire looks down at herself. She wears a black dress, elegant and simple, one that divulges distinctly more of her breasts and hips than she normally does at work. Did she choose it to impress David? Truthfully, he didn't enter her mind when she was putting on clothes; she considered only the importance of the event, yet perhaps the thought swam underneath. The feints and submerged gestures of dating do not yet feel natural; years of marriage allowed her to forget how easily new affairs start and stop, how an untested romance can dissolve quietly and without explanation. She dislikes the thought of playing this game again, and in tonight's circumstances it seems especially unpleasant. This is hardly the time to sort through her feelings for David. They are both adults. When he arrives they'll act the part.

Bernard rescues her from her thoughts. 'This way,' he says. 'I want you to meet these ones. Big donors, of course, but none of the usual foolishness. I think they're more to your liking.' Claire smiles and submits to the urgent tug at her elbow, falling into step with Bernard, and across the room she spots their quarry: a man about Bernard's age with a woman who could be a year or two younger than Claire. She smiles inwardly. Men remain a constant source of amusement. She cannot believe how a man of such age, something north of sixty, can appear in public with a woman – a girl! – so young. She would have thought men of that age would be more ill at ease about their bodies, the shrinking and withering, the wrinkles and the spots. How could he take off his clothes, and she hers, and he remain standing there with even a drop of dignity left in his heart?

Before they quite have reached the couple, Bernard leans in to whisper: 'David Kim isn't going to make it. He's caught a bug, it seems.' Claire looks quickly into his face, worried that he knows about her and David — would it matter if he did? — but the expression there reassures her that he intends only an innocent report on a colleague's whereabouts. Gossip about subordinates mercifully isn't one of Bernard's interests.

Introductions are made, after which Bernard, in his way, manages to slip off inconspicuously. He's a valuable commodity, and part of the reason he's offered up Claire is surely that he himself cannot be pinned down to one spot.

'It's a stunning piece,' says the man. His eyebrows jump like squirrels as he points to it with his glass.

Claire agrees. Sometimes the donors want commentary from her, a taste of the culture that she possesses and they must purchase in discrete lumps; others want not to be lectured, but listened to.

'Are you familiar with his other work?'

'Not all of it,' he says earnestly. 'I do like what I've seen. I've been thinking for some time of getting one of his myself, but nothing's come on the market I quite love. Of course Jenny has other opinions. She finds him too masculine.'

The girl says nothing, but the pause hangs there longer than it should, and Claire sees that she has stepped into one of the private eddies of their relationship, a surfacing difficulty. She interrupts it with a joke: 'If you're interested, I think we could part with this one for around thirty-one million.'

They laugh gently. He says, 'You must have your own thoughts about it.'

The usual phrases clutter her mind. She could close her

eyes and recite a publishable paragraph of commentary. But to give the appearance of deliberation she stares at the painting, as if seeing it for the first time. They are standing too far from the piece to discuss its finer details, and the man shows no interest in moving closer. Even across a room, though, it exerts a certain gravity. Its quality is beyond dispute.

But she has her doubts. For one thing, she worries about durability. Its title, *Century*, is both a promise and an expiration date. Caravaggio and Michelangelo still shake us, hundreds of years after their deaths, and even the cave paintings have a raw, lasting power. In five hundred years what will this piece look like? Art that lasts must leverage the power of symbols, the deep grammar of line and color installed in humans at birth; the images of *Century*, a mulch of the twentieth century, may, after worse and bloodier centuries have come and gone, pale next to more entrenched, enduring icons.

Claire ties off this reckless mental unspooling. The man and his girlfriend continue to wait for a response; he scans the room a little impatiently, searching for a graceful exit. She considers telling them what she's been thinking, just to see their reaction, but because it is easier she says what she could have said without ever opening her eyes.

They drift away. Immediately, she loses sight of them in the atrium, now full of people, people pushed even to its outermost edges. Its high white walls, and the vertiginous feeling they inspire, have always made her think of a cathedral, a building reaching without apology toward heaven. Chatter floats up to the rafters, soaring more than one hundred feet above them. She spots an art dealer she knows — they have met once or twice — but as she takes a step toward him she lands badly on her left foot and the four-inch heel under it turns awkwardly, wrenching her ankle. Cartilage and tissue throb angrily. No one has noticed. But the man she meant to speak to has fallen into conversation with three people she doesn't recognize. Keeping a careful grip on her drink, Claire slips off to the side, where there is a bench, and she sits and rubs the ball of her ankle as if cleaning a piece of glass. She finishes her drink. When she stands and tests her ankle it feels only a little sore, but she finds that she cannot bear the thought of making small talk for another hour. One of the waiters walks by and she snatches a canapé. Chewing the mouthful of dough and salty meat, and wishing she weren't, she decides that she can safely leave. She swallows. Halfheartedly, she looks for Bernard to tell him, and considers pleading illness until she remembers that David did the same thing. It doesn't matter, she decides. Bernard is, anyway, already off somewhere putting his thoughts in order before he speaks.

She feels better as soon as she steps into the gelid night: what a difference it can make, a sudden change in temperature. It will be a few minutes before the car she called arrives. Only now does she realize how warm it was inside, the heat collecting in her neck and cheeks, and she closes her eyes as the cold rinses it out of her. She just wants to be home. The earlier anxiety about David, and about Paul, returns only briefly; it slides away.

The car's here. Pale, fiery reflections swim through the licorice-black surface. It doesn't take long to reach her block, but the one-way goes against the driver, and he would have to circle around to pull up to her building. She tells him not to bother — she can manage half a block on foot. It isn't even eight o'clock and all she can think of is sleep. Maybe after taking off her shoes and changing into something more comfortable, she'll feel better. She'll cook something. Put on the TV. On the sidewalk behind her she hears footsteps, and the sound startles her — she didn't realize anyone was nearby. It's a young man. His head points downward, and he grips a brown paper bag. He doesn't wear gloves. He's just a delivery boy, walking slowly and shuffling his steps, and probably having trouble finding the right address. Claire has a mother's stab of worry: this young man, wearing only a light jacket, isn't dressed properly for the weather.

At the threshold of her building, not quite having summoned the energy to rummage in her purse for her keys, Claire pauses. She half expected to find Paul drunk and asleep on the step again. The delivery boy is a few doors behind her. He looks at the building in front of him, and at the one across the street; he takes a few paces in the other direction. She's surprised to realize that it is Paul she would like here, only to walk with her these last steps to her door, not David, not anyone else. She would have preferred not to know that. She wants to silence her mind. But she has to think of something. Her restless brain cannot keep quiet. A writer she once read likened the mind to a bowl, but this strikes her as false – a bowl can be emptied and cleaned and put back on the shelf. Some tap in her mind is always open, always running. Only at the end will it leave her alone. Even then it might not. Sometimes she thinks that it seems unlikely we die: such a voluble thing as a mind, surely, cannot simply be shut off. On a different night this might grant her some solace, her proof against death.

Around her the cold air closes its grip. Claire shivers, and hurries to find her keys.

He didn't keep track of how long he remained on the train. He changed lines several times, slicing briefly into Queens, and eventually disembarked in the low hundreds of Manhattan. In the harsh, unchanging light of the tunnels, time lost structure, and even though he checked his watch

Paul couldn't feel the meaning of the hours as they fell away. All afternoon and into the evening he then wandered on foot, shifting his path between the avenues, switchbacking along the cross streets, as the sky accelerated into darkness. He sat somewhere and bought a sandwich, but his appetite had deserted him, and he was able to finish only a few bites; so he went to a cafe and had a coffee, trying to kill the hours, even as he knew that there was no point: no hour would bring the waiting to an end. So he had another coffee, and another, and when he finally left his veins were tense and his eyes had trouble staying in focus.

In the wider city anonymity acts as a kind of shelter. Something in Paul sags at the thought; it is a desperate man who must depend on the safety of crowds. Terence has become the lump you avoid having a doctor look at. Finding himself near Central Park, he takes a seat on a bench and watches people emerge from the gloaming. Lamps, firm and white, dot the paths just within the walls, as even as items on a shelf; the deeper recesses — brown, black, purple — swell roughly.

It isn't his fault. He intervened to protect a stranger and next acted in desperation, on the wrong end of a lopsided fight, then only to save himself. Nor has he done anything, beyond the initial encounter, to provoke Terence, who in his obstinate pursuit is as unpersuadable as a wild animal. But he isn't. He is a person. He has his reasons. Without sitting him down and subjecting him to psychoanalysis, there's no way of knowing what misdirected neural traffic, what traumatic episodes and shaping incident, have created him. Was it a woman? The absence of a woman? Parental neglect? Poor environment? Damaged genes? It doesn't matter. Terence can't be fixed.

Inside his jacket Paul's phone vibrates. He reaches for it absently and answers without looking at the number.

No one's there. Then a woman's voice surfaces, so faint at first that he doesn't recognize it.

'Paul? He says . . .'

There are sobs, and then the sound of the phone falling.

'Claire? Is that you?'

'Paul,' she says when she has the phone again. 'Paul, he knows who you are. He says he knows you. Please, please hurry.'

He can't make out what she says next. Then, with a staticky rustle, she is gone. A new voice, a man's, comes on the line.

'Funny, I wouldn't of guessed you for a Paul.' In the background is the sound of glass shattering. 'Claire and me, we're just having a beer, talking about you. I'm a little clumsy, I dropped the bottle. I'll have to clean that up later, sweetheart. We'll wait for Paul to get here and give me a hand.'

His voice has grown distant: he's moved his mouth away from the phone and is speaking directly to Claire.

'What do you want?'

'You just better get over to your girlfriend's place before I get clumsy again and slice out her eyes.'

9

The taxi driver, braked at a red light, asks three times for the exact address before Paul, incensed at the man's poor memory, responds. He told him when he got into the cab, or at least he assumes he did. He boils inwardly with frustration. Up the avenue, as far as the eye can see, glows an endless hovering parade of red signals, crisp and clear in the foreground, and scuzzily indistinct further south. Midtown traffic rises to the level of moral atrocity. He feels the agony of ambulance drivers, immobilized in a tideless sea, staring into the indifference of hundreds of taillights, and considers abandoning the cab, running all the way to Claire's. But fifty blocks stand between here and there; he hasn't run that far in years. The cab sneaks ahead through another two intersections. At the next red light Paul's teeth clamp down automatically when the driver jerks to a stop. He should be using this lull to his advantage. He should make a plan of attack. But he has difficulty concentrating; the only coherent thought that will form is shame at how helpless he's become.

He tries Claire's phone; no answer. He briefly considers calling the police, but if they rush into the apartment, Terence may act rashly — he promised as much. Paul's one chance is to offer up himself and lure this maniac away from his wife. He doesn't know what happens after that. Traffic clears and the car begins to move. His heart tears itself apart as they approach Claire's block.

Paul thrusts two twenty-dollar bills across the divide, much more than is owed, and jumps out. In front of the building, he calls Claire's phone again: still no answer. The quiet of the street makes it impossible to think that anything is happening here. Someone comes out, and Paul uses his chance, squeezing in before the door can close. He climbs the stairs two at a time. Only when he reaches the apartment does it strike him that Terence might be armed; he may have a gun. Surely he knows how to get one on short notice. But the time for thinking, for hesitation, has passed. Paul tries the knob and finds the door slightly ajar. As he quietly pushes it open, he realizes that he doesn't know what to do with his hands, how to hold them, what posture to assume.

The room is dark; his eyes adjust slowly. Illumination comes only from a far doorway, where he can see a patch of tiled floor – the kitchen. Hardly breathing, Paul steers himself there, moving as quickly as he can while remaining silent, nearly silent. As he approaches he hears breathing, and, as it thickens and condenses, he recognizes the sound of quiet sobbing. Only when he's about to step into the room does he see how foolish he's been. Terence isn't going to wait in the light. This new fear starts as a little throb and then rises up, spreading under his skin, thrashing around in his blood. He turns abruptly. No one's there.

'Claire?'

In the other room, the sobbing rises in pitch, broken by loud moans. It is a mark of exhaustion, a sign of someone who has been crying a long time, who must use a certain amount of muscular effort to continue. Then the sound stops altogether. Paul steps inside. On the floor is a spray of green glass. A second bottle of beer sits on the table, open but still full. He scans the room, expecting Terence to come leaping from behind the door, from inside a cupboard. The air bristles with his presence. From a woodblock on the marble counter he pulls out a medium-sized knife; then he finds Claire.

She is a knot in the corner, a gnarl of anguish. She's wearing a coat and appears to want to swallow herself in it; with her head buried in arms and bent knees, she doesn't hear him. Paul, afraid to touch her, waits. Lifting her head from its nest she starts: on her face is a look of horror, as if she can see no difference between Paul and the man who was just here. He sets down the knife and helps her up.

'Where is he?' asks Paul. Every part of him is coiled, tight, hard. Claire makes no reply.

'Claire?'

'I don't know.'

'Where is he?'

'He left. I think he left.'

Paul steps into the darkened living room again, then makes a circuit of the apartment. He opens the closet in her bedroom. Terence is gone.

'Are you hurt?' he asks when he returns to the kitchen. He searches her for signs of physical vandalism. 'Did he do anything to you?'

She shakes her head, then says: 'He – he touched me.' With her finger, Claire marks a soft path from her eye's bottom pout to the corner of her mouth. Paul waits, and then places an arm across her shoulders.

They go to the living room. She sits on the sofa. He wanders around in search of the light switch, and when he looks at Claire, she offers no direction. He gives up, and, anyway, he can see well enough by the glow from the kitchen. The place looks nothing like those they shared during their years of marriage, and the years before that.

The furniture has the vague ordinariness of apartments in films. The art on the walls, which he didn't notice when he was here Sunday night, must have been acquired since the divorce. A pair of unwashed wineglasses stands on an end table.

They sit in the dark. Slowly she recovers her composure, and the story starts to come out. She held the front door for Terence, who because of the bag in his hand seemed to be a delivery boy, although she already felt a little wary of him, and when his footsteps followed her up the stairs, her wariness brightened into fear.

'I told myself I was being silly. I've lived in this city long enough not to become afraid every time I hear someone walking behind me.'

She reaches for one of the glasses on the table and drinks what's in it, screwing up her face at the taste, but drinking it all the same.

'When I tried to shut the door, he was there. His foot was. This heavy black boot, like a dog's snout, jammed into the door. I screamed, or I tried to, but he put his hand across my mouth. Suddenly we were in the kitchen. I was sitting. He put that bag on the table. I could hear glass inside, the sound of bottles, and even as this was all happening, I was thinking, "Why on earth has this man brought drinks into my home?" I had no idea what he planned to do.'

Claire turns the wineglass in her hand, then sets it back on the table.

'And he wouldn't stop talking.'

'What? What was he saying?'

Claire shakes her head, brushing away his question. 'He only left after Morris knocked.'

'Morris?'

'He lives upstairs. You don't know him. Sometimes he stops by after work. That man told me to stay here and answered the door. I was so terrified he'd do something to Morris. They spoke for a minute — I couldn't hear what they said. God knows what Morris thought. That man waited for him to go, then he left. Maybe he thought Morris would call the police.'

After a moment Paul asks, 'Did he have a weapon?'

'I don't know — I assumed he did.'

'No knife? No gun?'

'What is your point, Paul?'

He realizes how he must sound. 'I'm sorry.'

Claire waits before continuing. 'When he left, he said, "See you around." God, I can still hear him.' She closes her eyes as a shiver blows through her; one after another her limbs and features mutter with common disgust. 'I feel sick just thinking about it.'

She grows silent, then looks at Paul.

'I don't think I'll ever be able to get him out of my head.'

Ben listens to the sound of his wife showering. They got home an hour ago from Shabbat dinner with friends; feeling extravagant and insatiable at the end of a tiring — an unbelievable — week, he ate too much and drank more wine than he meant to, and now he feels the exhaustion sink through him. Next week has to be different. He has to make a change, find some other use for his time. Beth has left the bathroom door slightly ajar, which isn't a habit of hers, and the gap is wide enough almost to seem intentional. He considers crossing the room and closing the door, in case she merely forgot, but decides that it doesn't matter.

Rolling over in bed, he stares out the window, not really seeing. On the phone today his lawyer explained that the government will likely move forward with its case. He remains steadfast in his claim that events will unfold in Ben's favor, but his statements brim with the overzealousness of false confidence. Twisting the sheet between his hands, Ben fiddles with the notion of guilt, as if contrition can be a choice. Once again he can't feel it; it eludes him. He's no different from hundreds of other men, his deeds — small exchanges of information, routine chatter — indistinguishable from theirs. His happened to come to the government's attention at a bad moment. He had a piece of knowledge; he used it. That, he wants to tell his inquisitors, is how the world works. The city is full to bursting with rapists, killers, drug dealers, ordinary hoodlums, the jails aren't big enough to hold them all, and instead they come after him, a man with a career and a family, a belief in God, and want to make him pay. Because of them he may lose the ability to give his wife and son everything they deserve. For doing his job, for doing it better than most. For success. For that.

A moment elapses during which he is pinned on his back by the warm weight on his chest, the shock: he is a desperate man, he stands at the mercy of others. This was never supposed to happen. He meant to live ambitiously but carefully. A trial — even the threat of one and the agreement to a plea, if it comes to that — would be a slow-motion catastrophe. One way or another it will leave him reduced: if not with nothing, then certainly with less. He flops onto his stomach. It does nothing. The anxiety has entered his arms and legs, they twitch and crinkle, and he would like to be free of his body, the labor of his heart. The difficulty is that he's not moving, he's not doing anything. What can he do? That is the problem — there is nothing he can do.

He breathes through the fabric of the pillowcase, faintly sweet from the laundry — even the simple enjoyment of a simple thing is threatened; he cannot think of fresh laundry without thinking that he might lose such a privilege. Yesterday Paul provided him with an easy target for this frustration. It wasn't truly his brother's fault. For perhaps an hour last night after leaving the restaurant Ben was furious with him, but the feeling quickly subsided; it was replaced by something unfamiliar, a soft embarrassment at having allowed himself to be so easily provoked. He'll call his brother, if not tomorrow, then next week, maybe not to offer an apology, or to ask for one, but just to talk. It will be easier now, with their father finally gone.

He shuts his eyes, tries to push it all down, not wanting to burden his wife with his woes.

They had a small fight, if it can even be called that, on the drive home from dinner tonight. Voices weren't raised. Obliquely she mentioned once more her displeasure that he hasn't spent more of the day with her, since he isn't at the office, and he tried to explain, again, that it isn't easy for him, that he needs to boil off the adrenaline he'd otherwise use up at work. She's still upset, too, that he asked her not to come to the funeral — another exclusion whose necessity he had tried and failed to illuminate — which made it difficult to win her commiseration over Paul's behavior afterward. After a period of brittle silence, he made an attempt to change the subject, bringing up their son, whom he'd wanted to mention anyway.

'I spoke to Jake today. He aced his first paper in that European history class.' When his wife did not respond, he added, 'I miss him.'

'He visits too often,' she said. 'He needs to have his own life. We need to have our own lives.'

'I know, I know, I know.'

He is restless. He pushes back the sheets and glides from bed, and at the window his eyes snag on the view of the city. It would be possible to calculate down to the decimal point the value of this view when considered among the many other desirable elements — street address, floor space, ceiling height — that determined the price he paid for the apartment. That number wouldn't be a small one. He paid it to be able to look out upon the city that's his. He loves New York. At night the steel and glass vanish and all that remains is light. Towers blaze, vanilla and silver, and below them, like impure runoff, are lesser lights, rough and granular: the blue beer logos in bodega windows, the lamps coming on and off in taxis, the slurred glare of intersections. Further on is the great neon confusion of midtown, where digital semaphores flash and bicker, just below Central Park, that one reservoir of darkness. It is a view replicable nowhere else in the world. He is looking down at all of this, this city of light, but feels instead as if he is a former angel gazing up.

Just as he returns to bed, lying once more on his side, he hears his wife emerge from the bathroom, and, before he can turn to face her, she says: 'I'm sorry.'

Beth sits on the edge of the bed, still dressed in her robe. Her hair glistens under the light. Ben realizes that he didn't hear the hair dryer; when she showers before bed, his wife usually comes out of the bathroom already wearing her nightgown. Tonight, it seems, she's been diverted from long-held routine by the need to make peace. A pinch, a tiny convulsion, grasps him from within.

'I'm sorry too. Let's just forget it. We'll have lunch tomorrow.'

'I'd like that,' she says, touching his arm. Then, reaching behind her head and twisting her wet hair into a rope, she says, 'Stephanie's become a striking young woman, hasn't she?'

Stephanie is their friends' oldest daughter, a senior at Columbia. She made an appearance tonight at dinner, wafting through on a self-contained breeze, eating a few forkfuls and having a glass of wine before going off to rejoin her roommates, or work on her thesis, or see a film downtown; Ben wasn't really listening and cannot remember. His wife's question doesn't appear to require an answer. They might as well be talking about the weather, as far as he can tell, which is fine by him, an easy conversation to release the earlier tension.

'She must get such looks,' Beth continues. 'It has to be nice.'

'She isn't the only one who can get a look,' says Ben. He enjoys this, the gentle banter of people whose relationship can be measured in decades, and even feels at the corners of his eyes the first, soft tug of sleep. At last: the evaporation of difficulty, the return to normalcy. Thinking of the sturdy marriage he's been a part of putting together, he can picture the years ahead with uncomplicated pleasure.

She murmurs something he can't hear. He rolls onto his back. A flash of white billows into his peripheral vision. Beth has removed her robe, and wears nothing underneath. He watches her by a slight angle of his head: she is sitting with one knee hoisted up onto the bed, her skin still pink from the shower. She hides her eyes from him; they are looking down at herself. He can see the profile of one of her breasts, which have always been full but which the decades have made increasingly pendulous. When he senses melancholy or distress, he normally reaches out to touch his wife, but he finds he cannot.

He asks, 'You aren't wearing your pajamas tonight?'

Beth sits there as she releases a long, powerful breath, more than a sigh, and then draws back the covers on her side of the bed. She slides underneath them as if just now conscious of her nudity. 'I'm hot,' she says, rolling away to face the other side of the room, and Ben is suddenly wide awake, alert to his thoughts but unable to arrange them; he can't clear away the confusion of what has seemed like a very rapid shift in the marital weather. Ben dangles between thought and speech, suddenly in the fierce grip of an unfamiliar longing for the things he already has. He hears his wife's voice again.

'I'm tired. Will you please just put out the light?'

Moments pass. They do not move. Paul's arms make imperceptible adjustments as they find the old places: his body is remembering how to hold hers. In the weak light he can't read the titles on the bookshelf but recognizes most of the spines, their colors and dimensions, the white splinters of distress on the fatter paperbacks; the avulsion of his books from hers, after they'd lived in uncontroversial confusion for the better part of four years, had been one of the most arduous episodes of the divorce. After a while Paul's leg falls asleep. He delays, then unbends it, upsetting their pose on the sofa. Claire blinks, as if coming out of a long nap, and stands. She takes off her coat, underneath which she is wearing a flattering black dress, and Paul tenses at the sight of her bare arms, the delicate camber along each of her sides, the plush suggestion of her breasts. Was she on a date? He feels guilty for doing so, given all that has happened, but it is impossible not to stare. Without a word she crosses the room to the kitchen. The sound of the tap running. There he finds her, still trancelike, ruminating upon the broken bottle on the floor, perhaps unable to force away thoughts of how else the night might have ended. With her toe she pushes a piece of glass.

'Don't,' says Paul. 'Let me clean it up.'

He has taken control of the situation, it seems, but his confidence quickly shrinks after checking the two cabinets beneath the sink, then the closet next to the refrigerator, without finding so much as a dustpan. He looks around helplessly; Claire is unable to make words or even to look at him. Finally he asks: 'Is there a broom?' She sticks out her chin, in the direction of the living room, a vaguely pugilistic facial gesture that isn't usually part of her physical vocabulary. The closet there is carelessly full of the things that fit nowhere else. He takes the broom and returns to the kitchen, where he stoops to clear the glass; heat pours into his lower back until he can't maintain the position and, with an exhausted, half-dizzy swoon, falls to his knees to finish.

Paul feels himself go slack. At first he assumes it's the last dregs of fear evaporating. Because Claire doesn't speak, and because he has nothing to say, he can dwell within the silence of himself and more carefully palpate the emotion, testing its shape. It is hardly relief, but rather disappointment. His nerves are tight wires, anticipating combat, a mortal test – not broomwork. Paul didn't get the chance to prove himself. To save Claire's life. His arms shake a little. The smallest shards resist the clumsy bristles and impatiently he corrals them with the open edge of his hand. He's aware of Claire's presence above him, but she isn't quite there; she's more a nimbus than a person. He sweeps the remaining bits into the pan and in doing so presses down with his full hand, running it the wrong way over an innocuous-seeming pebble of glass. It draws blood. Only a drop, but at the sight of red Claire's senses return.

'It isn't serious,' says Paul. He shows her the cut.

'Let me get a bandage.'

'I don't need one.'

Claire takes his hand. The glass punctured the meaty ridge below his thumb; she presses down around the cut until a bright bead of blood wriggles out.

'See? It's nothing.'

'Still.'

He expects her to release his hand, but she doesn't. The air between them shrinks, he greedily breathes in the familiar scent of her hair, and his heart obliges: it is the response common to sex and danger – at once he can feel the movement of all the blood in his body, he's aware of every drop in his veins, a warm, weeping sensation cascading through him. He puts his hands on her arms, and they slide up to touch the cool, dry skin of her shoulders – it is almost painful how soft they are, and he's filled with delirious possessiveness. He holds her cheeks. Her eyes close, her lips drift apart.

They press together. A fumble of mouths. He touches her stomach but avoids her hip, where he knows she is ticklish. The kiss has no true pleasure in it, nothing sensual or passionate – only a shared desperation. Bursting with heat, sex, and terror, he murmurs the old three words, and at this Claire's fingers, which have been dragging at his face, relax, brushing him now with an almost maternal tenderness. He's kissing her without being kissed in return. He withdraws. It doesn't mean for her what it does for him: for her the kiss is only a necessary comfort, an uxorial reflex. They pull apart. She sits at the kitchen table, then stands and picks up the other chair. 'It doesn't belong there,' she says without quite addressing him. She places it on the opposite side of the table. 'He moved it when he sat down.'

On the white of her cheek is a fleck of red where he touched her. Paul sits, resisting the urge to reach across and wipe it away, recalling that Terence's hand was already there tonight. Without looking at Paul, she says his name, her voice faint and mildly scolding. Then: 'You still haven't told me. That man said he knew you.'

He gives her a puzzled look: he's forgotten that Claire knows nothing of the past week, knows nothing of the reason this man chose her apartment to burst into. She is suddenly very distant. The kiss they just shared could have been a month ago, a year. He offers an explanation of events, telling her what happened after he left her apartment on Sunday night, and describes Terence's intervening appearances. Claire struggles to restrain an expression of outrage. By his involvement, albeit accidental, in so awful an episode, Paul admits culpability for the man who just invaded her home; she watches him as if studying a stranger. At some point she interrupts: 'And you didn't call the police?' Paul chafes at her tone; it is disapproving to the point of condescension. He explains that in fact he did call the police, that it accomplished nothing and in his opinion calling again would have done as little good. When he finishes, she gets up to refill her glass. He's aware of the process at work within her, an attempt to restore an inner balance, her orientation in the world. Claire asks if he wants something to drink, then fills a glass for him without waiting for an answer.

'I'm sorry,' Paul says. 'I had no idea—'

She shakes her head. 'There's no point. We shouldn't.'

'Shouldn't?'

Again she shakes her head. Light bounces around the glass of water on the table. She slides away her hand when he reaches for it.

'Shouldn't what? Shouldn't kiss?'

Claire makes no reply.

'Shouldn't talk about us, then?'

'We weren't talking about us, Paul. There is no us.'

'Why did you invite me in last week?'

'God. Must you?'

'You expect me to pretend it didn't happen?'

'That would be easier, I think.'

'You're saying you regret it.'

'I'm not saying anything. Forget it. It doesn't matter.'

He wants Claire to meet his gaze. She doesn't. An impulse strikes him to reach over and lift his wife's chin, manually to fix her eyes to meet his. Instead, he stands.

'Are you leaving?'

'Are you asking me not to?'

She sucks in a long breath. Then she methodically collects the remaining open bottle, empties it in the sink, and returns it to the brown paper bag Terence brought. 'Please take that with you.' Paul's arm sags slightly as he accepts it. When he moves, the sound seems to come not from under his foot but from the other room. He looks at Claire, whose eyes are alive with dread. They speak in whispers.

'Didn't you lock the door when you came in?'

'I thought so.'

'Maybe I imagined it.'

Another sound comes from the living room. It isn't the imagination. Claire, operating evidently by instinct, a child-like part of herself taking over in the face of terror, reaches quickly to switch off the light — as if they can simply be made invisible — and plunges everything around them into darkness.

Paul moves first. But this initial act — a footstep — doesn't immediately suggest a next course of action. It compels him only to take a second step, and then a third, toward the black rectangle of the door, the threshold of the other room, in which the darkness thickens with unwelcome possibility. He looks back, trying to see Claire, but his eyes haven't adjusted to the sudden absence of light, and he makes the next step blind.

For a single, suspended moment, nothing happens. Then, bursting out of the darkness, a scribble of kinetic energy, Terence appears and grabs Paul by the jacket, throwing him halfway across the room with a twisting, apelike improvisation. Paul — lifted, light, a projectile — lands awkwardly on a low wooden table. Terence is quickly upon him: a blow across his face, followed promptly by another; high on his cheekbone the flesh immediately starts to swell, a concentrated purse of pain.

The pain means he is conscious. Throwing a punch feels cramped and hurried, but he lashes out with his fists, firing wildly in Terence's direction. It has the desired effect — Terence backs off — and, emboldened, he tries a kick. The weight of his shoe at the end of his leg feels promising, but as it pushes through air it meets no resistance: he misses. Hands lock onto his leg, below the knee, and drag him from the table in a single, gliding motion that ends with the back of his head on the hardwood floor.

'Don't you wish you hadn't fucked with me? Don't you, Paul?'

Terence stands over him, an outline, his face unevenly slashed across by shadows: his mouth emerges most prominently, a tense rictus above the white shelf of his chin. A second shape moves behind him. Terence turns before Claire can react, and Paul cries out in helpless anguish.

Terence strikes at her with an open hand. The motion is rash and imprecise, meant to deflect rather than injure Claire. She is hurled back against the far wall and Paul hears a crash of glass. When he looks he sees her slumped on the ground and, as if carried up by unseen hands, he stands, lowering his shoulder and leaning into the blow, driving this man away from Claire. They fall across the sofa; his legs go out from under him as he tries to keep a grip on Terence, to use this surge of anger. Paul is hit once, then twice. A mustardy odor fills his nose. He's prepared now for the sensation, the fat pulse of pain, and is able to answer in kind, aiming for the face, the bridge of the nose, places he has heard are especially susceptible to harm. It is difficult to move — they are pressed belly to belly, the cushions sliding and bucking beneath them as they struggle — and to concentrate on delivering blows while also avoiding them. He grabs

Terence and plants his left foot on the floor for leverage; then, in a single action, he stands while pulling his opponent to the ground, flipping him in the process, so that Terence lands in a prostrate position. But Paul hasn't got a clear sense of how to use this unexpected advantage, the set of instincts that would allow him to bring the moment to its resolution. When Terence tries to rise, he sits on him.

Below him the man twists and gropes around — a ghastly sensation of aggrieved, writhing muscle — as he tries to find some piece of Paul, a point of immediate vulnerability. He becomes aware of a tingling on his inner thigh, revolting because of its familiarity, its connotation of pleasure. Terence has wormed a hand around and now it slithers up Paul's leg, grazing the tightly bunched, ultrasensitive nerves there; in another second or two those fingers will have hold of his balls. Something crackles in his blood. Without thinking, he grabs Terence's head with both hands and lifts it up, allowing the spring of the neck to smash it back into the floorboards; he repeats the action, feeling a wild thrill of power, a freedom from consequence. He thinks once more of Claire: he draws up Terence's face again, this time simply by gripping the back of his head, and again delivers it in a stroke against the wood. By now he's ceased to struggle.

It's a temporary solution. Paul can still feel the gruesome heave of air going in and out. A single thought seizes him — the decisive thing. The knife. It would shift the balance of power, eliminating Terence's advantages in muscle, youth, temperament. By degrees he lifts himself off Terence, testing the response: the body below doesn't stir. He goes to the kitchen where it still sits on the counter. When he returns he sees Claire, fallen in a posture of incidental rest, and drops to his knees beside her, pressing his fingers into her neck. She has a pulse: firm spasms in the skin, one after

another, like a series of tiny gulps. A flutter of consciousness agitates her eyelids.

This dreamy little pause is a luxury Paul can't afford. He
has a fleeting awareness of the hostile presence above him
and then is lifted, as if rocked by a wave, hurtling backward, until the wall stops him. He's pinioned there under
the angled, inflexible slats of Terence's forearms. Hands
grasp at his face, each with autonomous ferocity, and he
shuts his eyes; sparks flare and dissolve against the black.
The powerful thumbs knead his cheeks, pressing against
the softest part, and inside his mouth he feels his own
spongy flesh squeeze between his teeth. The thumbs begin
to scale the bony ridge below his eyes. The pressure of a
scream mounts in Paul's throat, and at its point of release,
as he twists his neck in an effort to free his face, he makes
two tight jabs with his right hand, the hand that holds the
knife, which Terence couldn't have known he had.

Holding his stomach, Terence stumbles back. For Paul the
moment is a crush of visual information, of unfamiliar
sensation — it is a trembling below his skin like something
alive, separately sentient. His arm reaches outward, ahead
of his thoughts, and sticks the knife into Terence again.
Terence doesn't fall. Paul sticks the knife in again. A
delirious, spacious rage fills him. It is a sound inside the
dome of his skull, not quite a ringing, but something dull,
a heavy mechanical drone, an expanding warmth in the meat
of his face. The feeling is one of license: he can continue to
strike Terence as long as he wishes to, as if his hand is empty.
Terence wobbles forward, on his face an expression of perfect
surprise, as if it hadn't occurred to him before now that his
own existence, like that of every other living thing, would
be a temporary one. And even staggering, almost falling,
clutching at the cratered terrain of his front, he still appears
to believe, as does Paul, that he cannot die.

He lurches toward the door. He wants to get away; Paul should let him. But the flight of the command from his brain skips his logic centers and engages the muscles of his arm, arriving in his hand as a full-born impulse. Paul continues to plunge the knife into Terence even as he rattles the whole door in his panic, even as his feet scamper frantically and pointlessly. Paul stabs him again, and again, and again, and each time meets resistance – rib, spine, leather jacket. At last he finds a clean line into pure, pliant flesh. Still Terence won't fall. Finally, in a deliberate motion, Paul turns the knife, fixing it downward, and clocks it back, above his head, before swinging down savagely. The motion describes an arc, at the end of which is a spot on Terence's back, beneath the blond ellipse of his head, between the wings of his shoulder blades. Terence's hands, which have been struggling with the doorknob, slip away, and his body slides down the door, forced briefly into the curve of a feather.

At first Paul does nothing. He waits, frozen, expecting Terence to stand. Then, taking his jacket, Paul pulls him away from the door and turns him over – already the body seems to have gathered an immense additional weight, as if at the moment of death something actually entered rather than left it. He wants to see the eyes; he wants them to be shut, proof that Terence won't move again. But they hang open – they performed their work right up to the final stroke of his heart. They have a waxy, unfocused luster like new marbles and across each appears a bleak, guttering image, an animation of the living world projected onto a dead surface: the nearest window and, beyond it, a sharp night sky. Lights flicker and drift. Paul, peering closely, can even see his own convex reflection, powerful and disquieting proof that a man's death does not halt the rest of it – that we die one at a time.

Small details briefly seem important; he notes the hair on dead knuckles, the rubbery Adam's apple lodged in the dead throat like a cork. In death, young and pale-haired, incapable of working his features into that cocky menace, the insignia of threat, Terence appears gentle, even boyish. When Paul steps back, other circumstances assert themselves — plain, vital facts. For one thing, he's still holding the knife. Patches of blood blackly stain his pants and more cling to his front. Blood sticks to the doorknob and on the door itself, against which Terence must have pushed his stomach as he tried to escape, hang a few shoddy lines, like the shreds of a flag. And there's more — it spreads heedlessly across the floor. Then he sees that Claire has risen to her feet: she appears not to be hurt. But on her face is an expression like none he has ever seen her make, even during their episodes of greatest marital agony. She looks at the body blocking the door, then once more at Paul. Though he cannot regard himself, he doesn't have to — it crashes down on him nevertheless, what she sees, the recognition of everything that he no longer is.

The sensation of the knife in his hand is odd, a firm object and a common one, but one whose weight and balance now seem totally foreign. And there's Claire, standing in the dark: she is a pair of damp, iridescent eyes, bobbling with horror. He would like to hold her. To be held. Against the silence he hears the distant hum of traffic; of lights; of machinery; the ambient din that in other circumstances provides comfort, proof that the human world is still switched on, people are still coming and going, wanting and striving. Out of the general static of his thoughts emerges a vivid, pulsing point: *It isn't what I meant to do.*

This is what he would like say to her, to make clear that he's not — that he should not have been — a killer. Everything accelerated in that instant. Even now his breath saws at the air; a lifted, ecstatic feeling, like trapped gas, collects across his chest. He recognizes the need for choices, for action. This is an occasion for rationality, for the razor's edge of lucid decision-making, yet the only thoughts that will form are glossy bubbles, melting clumps. Heat flushes through him.

First he would like to put down the knife. An unpleasant, granular feeling chafes around the handle – dirty, harsh, like sand stuck against perspiring skin – and he can see how the weapon upsets Claire; ten minutes ago it was an ordinary kitchen knife. The threat is over, and she hasn't come to him. Not wishing to contaminate another surface of the apartment, he returns to where Terence lies and, in a motion of stupid delicacy, places the knife upon him. The blood, a body's worth of blood, a deep, dark pool, spreads unevenly under Terence; only the doormat, the bristles at its edge stained and wilting, stops its progress and prevents it from leaking into the hall. He moves away. Now he can go to Claire; now he can comfort her. His heartbeats are airy and light – each skips through his veins like a polished stone on water. Hers, too, must have a strange rhythm, that much he knows: this kind of fear doesn't go on and off at a snap; it will take time to ebb, bathwater struggling down a clogged drain. Yet the absence of the knife seems to have had no effect whatsoever. Each step toward her causes Claire to make one in retreat.

'It's over. You're safe.' He has to say something, and these words are as good as any. At the end of his arm, half raised, his fingers waver in a motion of reaching, asking. She withdraws further.

'Claire.'

Even the pronunciation of her name qualifies as contact for which she is unprepared. It acts as confirmation that it is indeed she, here, in the middle of this nightmare. She shakes her head violently, eyes closed. Seeing is an affliction — she won't even look anymore. At all of it, the body, the chaos? Or only at him?

'Do something,' she says, and he understands. The body seems to poison the air. But it is difficult to reconstruct the last ten minutes. Once more he surveys the room as if to confirm the reality of it. The body. The blood. It did, all of it, happen.

At last a practical phrase comes to him: *self-defense*. It has the soothing power of a lozenge. He says it aloud: 'Self-defense.' Claire's eyes briefly flicker, open, shut again, her look one of skepticism and residual terror. She watched it happen: now, with closed eyes, she rejects the plea. Claire, who once would have done anything for him, whom he believed he was saving. Was that actually what he believed? He would like it to be so, but he has trouble recollecting whatever threads of thought tightened within him during those last, cramped minutes. His mind writhes. It's impossible to find the honest version. Terence invaded the apartment, but he also tried to leave, and it was Paul who introduced the weapon, who raised the stakes. And Claire won't let him come near her: that one fact constricts him with a strong, accusatory grip.

More time goes by. The blood continues to spread. He wishes she would speak, even to say 'I hate you' or 'Go away.' Those at least would be expressions of emotion aimed at him. But she only cowers in the corner. Paul wants to tell her that she needn't be afraid, that he isn't going to hurt her, but to give voice to this is to admit that she appears to think it. He'll call the police. They will come and remove both him and the body. It can all be sorted out. He can be exonerated. Terence almost certainly would have killed him. Does that excuse the zeal with which he delivered those final blows? Even Terence would have preferred to go on living.

Paul takes out his phone and opens it. Claire hears: she watches him. It is clear that she has no idea what he plans to do, that she wants only to find out; if he's placing a call, a resolution may soon arrive. But by opening her eyes she has made him greedy for her attention, and he stops.

She asks, 'Who are you going to call?'

He makes no reply. The phone is open, the first digit is struck. Paul stares back at Claire, who shivers a little, clutching her bare shoulders, though it isn't cold. Actually, he realizes, it is quite hot in the apartment, an uncomfortable, downy closeness in the air. She won't come to him.

On the screen of his phone it waits, the nine, like a lower-case g, curled and innocent, for the hard double slash of the eleven that follows.

'I don't think we can call the police.'

'You,' she corrects him. 'You did this.'

What stops him from making the call? Claire, for one thing: even if he can't now cross the distance between them, the consequences of calling would pull him further from her. And he has the unfamiliar thought that there are pieces of his life he doesn't want disrupted. Had this happened a week ago he might not have cared, it might have been a relief to get hauled off by the police, but now he has a chance to write a book people will read, he has a chance to bring his brother back into his life. Like a child staring through a toy store's window, he gazes upon these things: bright, tangible, and just beyond his reach. He has chances. He has reason to want again.

He shuts the phone.

It makes a loud clap against the silence; Claire winces. He doesn't know how much time has passed since he killed Terence. When he next catches her eye, he replaces the self-pitying expression with one meant to impart decisiveness, and he sees that she plans to let him dictate the course of action. But she yields in a way that suggests simple fatigue, even submission. And she is – yes – she's also afraid of him.

'What are you going to do?'

Paul knows the answer; he sees no other choice. He hesitates, swallows, then opens the phone again and dials.

Ben picks up on the fourth ring. Paul hears in his voice an uncharacteristic note of concern, one that rapidly thins into a familiar, exhausted anger.

'Christ – Paul. I thought you were Jake. I was worried something had happened.'

'Something did happen.'

'Can't this wait until morning?'

'Please, Ben.' Paul's voice must strike the uppermost register of desperation, because his brother doesn't get off the line. 'I need your help. I need you to come.'

'Are you insane? Now?'

'You have to drive.'

Ben says something indistinguishable, and Paul realizes that he's speaking to Beth. 'I'm in bed. We were asleep.' There's a long pause. 'Paul,' he says, his voice gentler, drained of irritation, 'can't this wait? It's the Sabbath.'

'No,' says Paul, feeling something within him collapse. 'No, you need to come now. He's dead. I killed him.'

Waiting, Claire and Paul don't speak. They remain with the body but do not approach it, by silent agreement standing as far away from it as they can; from Claire's position it is probably not possible to see it. He washes his hands; for the time being he must live with the blood on his clothes. At some point he tries to go to her, but the reaction is unambiguous. 'Please – don't touch me.' He obeys, realizing that he expected as much. After a while, since there's no reason not to, he sits in a chair; she doesn't leave her rigid watch at the far side of the room and keeps the lights off. There are things Paul would like to say, but now that he's made a decision, his thoughts again have a rootless drift. When Ben arrives, Paul has to move Terence before he can open the door for his brother. The body is incredibly heavy, and he shunts it merely the minimum distance demanded by the situation, leaving it up against the wall, almost in a sitting position. Limbs and neck slouch at unnatural angles. It is behind the door, and thus out of Ben's line of sight when he enters. Instead he takes in the bedlam of the apartment: magazines spread across the floor like a folded hand of cards; the confetti of crushed glass at the base of the shelf; the cushions flung from the sofa. With his first true step into the room the heel of his shoe gives a small whine as it slides along the slick floorboard, then a light sucking sound as it peels up from the blood. Shifting to the left, where more waits, he only exacerbates his predicament, and in a quick, automatic motion he hurls the door shut behind him. It slams into the hall. Only then does he see the rest of it — the blood on the handle, on the door itself, and there, the reason for coming, the body. It is enough to halt him in his tracks, but by then it is too late: the blood is on him: he's standing in it.

Ben composes himself and moves to look more closely at the body and its wounds. 'Christ,' he says. 'Christ.' Ben stares at the body with glazed eyes, which, looking across Paul's shoulder, snap again into focus — Claire. It has been three years, and in spite of the present scene the social moment brims with quiet strain.

'Claire.'

'Ben.'

Their voices break the trance that has settled around them like dust. Ben wears an expression that doesn't lend itself easily to interpretation. Paul is out of options; he isn't. He could walk away, or even call the police himself. These seem to be the most likely outcomes. Finally he asks what happened. Paul explains, or tries to – he speaks too quickly, misremembers. Claire offers no help. At a few points Ben asks questions; Paul does his best to answer them. Ben, who is breathing heavily but otherwise seems impressively calm, takes a few steps around the room and by a gesture of his head makes clear that he is aware of the footprints he leaves. It isn't clear what he plans to do, but he hasn't left, and his face shows a quality of calculation as he analyzes the state of affairs he's come upon – and, doubtless, its consequences. And then he quivers slightly, like the shudder, the long creak, the buckling of wood and iron and plaster in a condemned building at the instant before it falls. With the flash of epiphany Paul sees what is happening: his brother is going to act irrationally, to step out of character: he isn't going to walk away. He's going to help. Despite the unlawfulness and the deep ignominy of the task at hand, Ben's eyes are lit, a mind at work: he is plotting, arranging, anticipating. Of the two of them, he's unquestionably the more fit to manage an extraordinary situation, even one not of his own making. This isn't his duty, yet, as Paul watches, he is strapping it on. It is what he hoped for, but Paul finds himself crushed all at once by a deep sense of shame, a massing dread, at winning Ben's consent for the endeavor. The feeling is one he knows too well, the disgrace of burdening others.

'We need a sheet,' says Ben, looking at Claire, who goes into the bedroom: her response is nothing like that which she gave Paul. He finds the switch that Paul could not and puts on the light. A moment later Claire emerges carrying a crisply folded deck of white sheets; it might be all the linen she has.

'Gloves,' he says. He already wears them; Paul doesn't. Once again, Claire vanishes before returning with a pair, black and cotton, the kind that stretch to fit any hand and are usually worn by children.

'Did you touch him anywhere?'

Paul thinks. 'His jacket.' Ben looks at Paul until he understands. Pulling on the gloves, he stoops to wrestle Terence's jacket off him; he has to pull out each dead arm as the fibrous straps of unconsenting muscle roll and flop in his hands. Finally the jacket comes off – leaving only an undershirt that exposes two bare arms, sleeved in tattoos – and Paul sets it on the floor.

'Put the knife in that,' his brother says. 'We'll get rid of it on the way.'

Ben's movements have a decisive economy. He disappears for a moment into the kitchen, from which comes the sound of water running, and returns with a clump of wet paper towels in his fist. He spends a moment cleaning the blood from his shoes; when he is finished he holds a crumpled ball, dark as a cherry. Then he opens one of the sheets, shaking it until the whole white cape billows out; a bulb of air swells in the middle, and it falls with the lazy swoon of a parachute. Paul feels sapped of willpower, ready to do as his brother says. 'Get the legs.' Ben lifts the shoulders and together they hoist the body. It isn't especially large, but the entire middle sags between them, heavy as cement; the arms dangle. They work to balance the body, to account for its irregular distribution of weight, its odd stray parts. They carefully lower him onto the sheet.

Drawing a long breath, Paul lets the weight drain from his fingers. He hears his brother's voice: 'We have to wrap him now.' Paul doesn't move. Instead he watches Claire; it isn't clear to him what he wants to say to her, or what he wants her to say to him. Claire, too, looks directly at him, but it is the gaze one makes across a distance. Again his brother speaks, quiet and firm: 'I certainly don't intend to do this on my own.' Paul bends and takes a leg into his hands. Ben stops to correct him, suggesting a better method of wrapping the body. They begin again.

It has a haphazard appearance. The white sheet, mottled with soily blossoms of blood, looks loose, ready to fall apart. Ben considers this. Finally he says they aren't done; they need garbage bags. 'Black ones,' he says. Claire fetches them, and the brothers, moving faster now, almost a rivery feeling pulsing under their movements, hasten to finish. It looks ready to travel now, even if, to a witness, its contents would be unmistakable.

Claire lives on the second floor. All three gather by the entrance and listen for any hint of movement in the hall. There is only silence. When they open the door the light that greets them is grisly and bright, publicizing everything it touches; the idea of transporting a body through this exposed, echoing space assumes an extra grade of peril. It would take only one tenant coming home at the end of the night to raise the alarm. But they are committed: the body is wrapped, the car parked downstairs. Ben nods, and together they lift it.

As they step into the hall, carefully avoiding the slick of blood, Paul looks once more at Claire; she returns the look, and says nothing. With legs and arms and back tense from exertion, he can hold onto only one coherent thought in the few seconds their eyes are joined: a wretched awareness that it would be easier not to see each other again, not ever, a thought ordinarily enough to burst his heart but which is made even worse by the knowledge that nevertheless they must—that the work of cleaning the apartment is his responsibility, one he will later undertake as an obligation, a matter of fealty, of hopeless principle. The brothers are clear of the door; she shuts it behind them. 'I'll go first,' says Ben, backing toward the lip of the stairwell. They begin the descent. At the turn in the stairs they must lift the body and rotate it like a long piece of furniture. From a hall above spill the spreading, layered echoes of a door shutting. Paul freezes, but Ben shakes his head — no point in stopping. They must go on. Suddenly they are outside. Noise froths near the bar at the end of the street, where voices slosh alcoholically back and forth. But Friday-night drunks make poor witnesses, and in any case the brothers have chosen a good moment: nobody's coming from either direction. The car is parked away from the light. Using a button on his key ring, Ben unlocks the trunk: it springs open with a ghastly exhalation. They stand there as Ben uses his foot to push to the back a shovel he must keep in the car for winter. Even then, it seems, the body isn't going to fit, but, with a certain amount of bending and coaxing, it does. Ben slams the trunk. The sound ricochets off nearby buildings, then dies.

10

His brother doesn't say where he plans to go and Paul doesn't ask. They drive north. They follow the edge of the water, just as the English must have done, and the Dutch, and before them the Indians, and who knows who else. The car's wheels sing crisply along the F.D.R.; white-paneled trucks rise in the rearview mirrors like lighthouses, then fall away. The skyline bulges and narrows above them like a cemetery of giants. The East River is as black as oil, and on its pitted surface floats a swaying, reflected version of the same city, the same swirling lights. A city of millions, New York, like an experiment in the limits of density, the level of proximity ordinary people can stand. It is a city of everything, of every possibility. Paul stares. Windows — some lit, some dark — stare back, and he feels modest, watched.

It is precisely for this reason, he knows, that Ben plans to take them away from the city. He drives at a moderate speed. Traffic is thin on the expressway, and they move easily. Ben still hasn't given a hint of his thoughts. The light across his face changes as they drive under streetlamps, shadows slicing it in different directions. At a glance Ben's features appear typically stony and, tonight, slightly ashen. But Paul notices a new habit of his eyes, an inability to stay focused on the road ahead; Ben isn't normally a man who has trouble holding a steady gaze.

'Are you okay?' asks Paul, aware of how stupid the question sounds.

'I'm just trying to figure out what I tell Beth when this is over.'

They continue in silence, pushing through the darkness between cities. For miles the highway is changeless. Sulking trees; glittering, stoic road signs. The proud thrum of the engine. The hushed fizz of tires on pavement. In the lane of oncoming traffic orphaned headlights blaze into view and a pair of red embers recedes. Paul loses track of time.

Like an outpost in the desert, a ragged, spectral glow materializes a few hundred yards ahead. Road work. Men in bright orange safety vests walk here and there — dozens of them, moving with the fractured slowness of dots on a radar screen. A vent of rubber cones constricts traffic into a single lane. The lonely highway swiftly becomes crowded; cars that had been pushing dully through the night in contented anonymity now line up with the intimacy of teeth in a zipper. They adopt the obedient rhythm of vehicles approaching a checkpoint. A police cruiser idles nearby, its revolving blue and red lights slicing the air like the blades of a helicopter, and an officer wearing black gloves and a heavy cap nonchalantly controls the flow of automobiles. Paul looks down at his own clothes, the spots of blood in his lap and on his front, which in poor light appear colorless, merely dark. He tries to think of them as blotches of spilt water. Work has stripped away the smooth grain of the road and made it uneven; the tires growl and slip. Ben eases off the gas, and both men hear the body change position in the trunk.

They are about to pass through the policeman's watch. Paul's stomach hurts. He looks quickly at his brother, seeking reassurance, but Ben's face doesn't yield to the moment's tension, its terrible element of chance. How easily the car could get a puncture on asphalt littered with construction equipment. A careless driver might knock them from behind. Ben seems oblivious to these scenarios. The only sign of his anxiety is the strength with which he grips the steering wheel: the section of its arc between his hands looks like the bow of a stick he intends to break in two.

They come to a complete halt as a gang of men, ferrying a long object of indeterminate purpose, cross the road and two cars ahead the policeman holds up a hand against traffic. The men are startlingly near, wearing haggard faces, and around them the air churns with breath. Powerful white lamps give their orange vests a crystal radiance, while behind them the night is as still as a photograph. Then they're across. Paul continues to stare until, underneath him, he feels the car gather speed, and once again he and Ben are on their way.

When they go over the state line into Connecticut, Paul looks expectantly at Ben, who senses his brother's thoughts and shakes his head. He explains that he wants to get beyond New Haven before stopping. 'I know the area. Friends live up here.' It seems like a long way to drive but Paul accepts this without protest; he isn't even sure on what grounds he would disagree with his brother, and has only a vague sense that it is a mistake not to rid themselves of the body sooner. Whether or not the decision is a misguided one, he's just grateful not to have to make it alone.

'Thank you,' he says. 'For doing this.'

The ensuing silence is far from companionable. Paul turns away and regards his own sparse reflection in the window. It has the thinness of a pencil drawing, a glimpse of an older self, a harbinger: of tired, scraped-out eyes; of delicate and graying hair; of sunken cheeks, bleached skin, cracked teeth. It comes and goes with the light, like a flickering spirit.

Ben applies more pressure to the gas.

New Haven glows ahead. Living in New York makes one forget the smallness of other cities: as quickly as its lights hatch into view, New Haven is gone, remembered only by the rearview mirror, blurry and quivering, like a rack of votive candles. Not until they are through the city does it occur to Paul that Ben's son is at Yale, that they were only a few turns from the building in which he sleeps. Though he doesn't acknowledge it, Ben knows it, too. With awful clarity and a flash of self-pity, Paul, finding it difficult to look at him again, realizes what he's asked of his brother.

He says, 'You didn't have to come.'

The statement is meant as a question. Ben doesn't speak, but his face, uncharacteristically adrift and washed of all assurance, nonetheless makes the answer perfectly clear: he doesn't know why he chose to help. Paul nods slowly; his lips part, but the apology he wants to give doesn't come out.

After driving for another half an hour Ben signals and takes an exit, and they leave the highway, as around them the road becomes darker, the objects at its side black and fixed.

They are alone on the road now. It took almost no time to remove themselves from the main arteries of traffic; they drive along a simple two-lane route, among only the trees, whose skeletal boughs reach wearily across their path. Paul gets the feeling that soon Ben plans to stop. He does, at a point of visible thickening in the roadside copse, and they sit for a minute, the engine idling, as if waiting to begin a conversation. 'This is the place I had in mind,' he says.

Paul makes no reply; Ben opens the door. Ribbons of sound, slipping in through the broken seal, split apart the silence, then destroy it altogether. The wind. The hard, zinclike odor smolders inside his nostrils.

'There's a turnoff,' says Ben, 'up ahead. It would get us

deeper into the trees, but I don't want to drive on dirt – tire marks are as bad as fingerprints. We'll have to get rid of our shoes, too.'

These details of planning, which would never have occurred to Paul, renew his gratitude for the presence of his brother, who, wasting no time, opens the trunk. It is still there, bathed in a light as dark as yolk; at the ends the surplus corners of the garbage bags are slack, innocently bunched, and elsewhere the material is stretched to an ironed smooth-ness, a menacing tension in the plastic suggesting the contours of its contents. Following Ben's lead, Paul takes one end; they lift, treating their cargo gently, as if afraid to damage it. Paul's legs become spongy. He has to grasp the ankles very firmly, squeezing hard enough so that they don't slide out of his hold; it requires immense concentration to keep the tendons taut in his fingers and wrists. The plastic is surprisingly slick and wants to slip away. It seems that he won't be able to go on, but then Ben begins to move.

At the side of the road is a knee-high metal barrier; they step across in unison. Ben, who carries the heavier end and walks backward, is patient, waiting to make sure that Paul has control before proceeding. They go on, faster now; navigating the woods and the uncertain terrain, they begin to move in sympathy with each other.

Branches appear like dark diving birds, rasping the side of Paul's face, and with every step he accumulates a disas-trous clumsiness. He trips on an exposed root and swears. The word sounds unusually loud. How little noise there is, silence congealed a palpable substance: a true quiet, the kind not found in cities. Ben glares at him across the length of the body.

'We need to get,' says Ben, pausing awkwardly for breath, 'far from the road.'

Paul nods, though he doesn't know how much longer he

can keep up his end. He's holding the body much lower than he was when they took it from the car. His back is on fire, his knees creak and ache. Each step leaves him freshly aware of this or that obscure joint and tendon. Sweat pours out, finding clefts in his back, collecting between his hip and the waist of his pants. Groping to regain his grip on the body, he thinks of Ben, his extra twenty years. Paul can hear the severity of his brother's breathing, which has grown in urgency over the last few minutes, and until now he hasn't thought of Ben's heart, of its fragile condition and the punishment it must be taking. Perhaps it's even worse than Ben let on — at any moment his brother could succumb to a feverish quaking in his chest. Paul watches him closely, inspecting him for a sign of trouble, a look of anguish.

A few feet on, Ben stops. Paul braces himself for the worst. His brother doesn't collapse. Instead he looks once over his shoulder and says: 'Here.' They are far too exhausted to respect their cargo, to lower it solemnly. It falls, landing on a bed of frozen leaves — the leaves of this year and the year before that, all the leaves the ground has not yet digested, a decaying canvas in gangrenous shades of green and brown. The smell rises heavily, faintly sweet. They have almost no light.

Ben says, 'I have to get the shovel from the car.'

'Shouldn't I come?'

'Stay here. Otherwise we might not be able to find it again.'

'How are you going to find me?'

There's a pause. 'Just wait here.'

Paul does as he's told. The stripes of muscle on his back, the cables that stretch under his arms, aren't able to release the coiled tension of exertion: his body won't forget the weight of the one it has been carrying. Obscenely, he feels hungry. He can't remember when he last ate; thoughts of food harass him. Time passes. He worries suddenly that his brother doesn't plan to return. Paul listens closely for the sound of a car's engine. He hears nothing, but in the absence of evidence to the contrary, it is difficult to imagine that Ben will reappear — Paul has been left alone with the body of the man he killed. Against his side he feels the vibrations of his phone, and he fumbles through buttons and pockets and the folds of his coat. Flipping it open, he puts the phone to his ear and says, 'Hello? Hello?' No one's there. It wasn't Ben's voice he was hoping to hear, he realizes, but Claire's, and when he looks at the screen he sees that it isn't a call at all, only the phone's warning that its battery is about to die. The plastic at his feet snickers in the wind. The phone sits in his hand like a stone. He hears, at last, the nearby crunch of crusty earth.

'Ben?'

Gripping the shovel by its throat, he appears. Without a word he stops alongside the body and drives the spade into the ground, tearing up a hunk of earth. He pauses to straighten his glasses before bringing down the shovel again; the motion is abrupt and hugely violent. He digs. Against the resistance of cold dirt his movements grow ragged. He attacks the ground with a rough determination; by the gathering choppiness of his breathing Paul knows the strain this exercise is putting on his brother. Ben stoops to pull out and move away a large rock that obstructs the shovel. He seems to have little regard for the mess, getting himself dirty with surprising carelessness; but Paul's brother has always believed that something within himself is fundamentally clean. Paul steps forward, arm outstretched, offering to take the shovel. Ben's face is glassy with sweat. He does nothing at first. He breathes heavily and looks at Paul with obscure eyes. At last he gives it up.

Ben has split apart the top layer of earth, but Paul's first attempt to deepen the hole goes badly; the shovel punches through only a few inches of dirt and his bones clang painfully from the shock. The digging grows easier once he knows what to expect, and he finds a cadence; the work becomes mindless. Vaguely he senses Ben's nearby presence, and it makes him slightly self-conscious, his brother assessing the quality of his effort; Ben says nothing. After forty-five minutes of steady labor, Paul has stripped from the earth a hole maybe three feet deep, which appears to be about the size they need, though he can't stop himself from worrying that it isn't enough. Soreness condenses in his shoulders. He smears the dew of sweat across his forehead and opens and closes his hands, trying to stretch out the ache of the shovel's handle.

Ben watches him, mouth clamped in an impatient half-scowl.

'This is taking too long,' he says.

They stand in position, one at each end of the body, and lift it up. When it's directly above the hole, the body simply tumbles in; it fits. Paul stares at it, unable to move, until startled by the sensation of a hand on his upper arm: he turns and looks into his brother's face, a face disheveled by sweat and exertion, which even in the dark shines with a pink, athletic hue. But the expression there isn't easily categorized – it isn't unkind, nor is it necessarily fraternal or consoling. Ben, after holding this pose for a moment, takes back his hand.

Paul makes no effort to take over as Ben retrieves the shovel and fills the hole again with dirt. It is a much quicker process than the digging and soon the ground is level again. They gather leaves to cover the empty space; the excess dirt they scatter around. They step back and evaluate their work: the ground is artificially level, in a plot of otherwise wild, unused earth, but it would be difficult for a casual observer to realize what lies beneath the soil in this desolate, arbitrary place. They could not have done better.

Claire goes to the twenty-four-hour Korean grocery store and leaves with two plastic bags stretched almost to breaking: sponges, liquid soap, steel wool, Ajax, carpet cleaner, glass spray, paper towels, a six-dollar mop. It was obvious that she had been crying, but the man was kind enough not to say anything. The weight of the bags feels solid – a familiar thing, cleaning – but even before she reaches her apartment, as she climbs the stairs, as she pictures the scene there, a sense of impossibility fills her movements. The bags tug at her fingers and the feeling of encumbrance travels up her arms, pressing down on her shoulders, her back, even the top of her skull. Instead of getting to work as soon as she's inside – the blood on the floor seems even darker now – she drops the things on a table and goes to the couch, although to sit down she first must fix the cushions.

Claire closes her eyes; she needs to concentrate. It is easier to think now, with that man gone, with all of them gone. The pain of sanity returns, the last, cool numbness leaves her, and with her eyes closed she can't prevent impressions from forming there, highly vivid and burning with acrylic brightness. In the dusk of her eyelids the reenactment plays in silent, wretched detail. Paul's face was abstract and ghost-like, and before he killed that man his eyes flashed with a rough glow – it was desire, he was enjoying the manual sensation of plunging a knife into another human being. She doesn't want to have these thoughts, but she knows what she saw.

And then, when it was over, Paul, staring at her with loose wild eyes and heaving monstrously with breath, told her he didn't want to call the police. She consented – but for the life of her she can't remember why. She was unable to speak:

205

to put the signature of her own decisions on the event. An anesthesia of shock immersed her as she watched Paul use the knife, and it lingered as events gathered momentum around her. She became more and more numb. Ben asked for things; she fetched them. There is perhaps another reason for her acquiescence to Paul: she was terrified of him. With a tight jerk of her neck Claire looks once more at the blood. Will it even wash off? Given a wet sheen by the shadows, the bags of cleaning supplies hunch on the table, slouching and losing form like a pair of crumbling sandcastles. They seem unequal to the task; thirty-five dollars and eighty-seven cents' worth of chemicals couldn't possibly undo tonight's events. Her participation has been passive until now. She watched, she allowed. Applying herself to the job of scouring away blood is altogether a different order of engagement.

Her head hurts. She bites at a fingernail, wishing she had access to a voice other than her own, this useless, cluttered hum. Amazing, how quickly Paul rejected the involvement of the police — it seemed almost reflexive. What happened, what she watched, was much too large to be handled by those untrained for the task, not to pass through the machinery of authority. Civilization has established standards of behavior, reasonable expectations of its members, a mutually beneficial collective bargain. It could have protected Paul — people act unpredictably in moments of extreme anger or terror. Tonight can't be undone, but it could have been explained, absolved. By now Paul's actions have certainly crossed some threshold of criminality. Why did she let him convince her not to call the police, forcing her thoughts onto the same, irrational frequency, making her an accomplice?

It isn't that she has any sympathy for the dead man. When Paul asked what had taken place she supplied an incomplete version. The rest was simply too terrible to experience again, even as language. What did she tell Paul? Something about that man touching her face. That much is true. But it wasn't the end. He stood behind her, like a dentist, while she sat in a kitchen chair. She did not and could not move. Everything inside her trembled and twanged. Beer from the broken bottle made a warm scrim around them, and he'd been drinking before he arrived; the smell fell heavily from his mouth whenever he spoke. When he reached out, from behind, and rested a finger against her cheek, her entire skin leapt. With a finger, its dirty, ragged nail, he traced a line down her cheek, hewing to the ridge of bone beneath the skin. It moved in blurry proximity, a dark thing just below her eye, like an insect she couldn't swat away. Everywhere he touched, her skin registered the fingerprint, the oils, even once he'd moved on. A long, ribboned trail tingled across her face. He slowly brought the finger to the corner of her mouth, where she felt, just slightly, a pressure on her lips that forced the flesh inward, against her front teeth. The other hand held her chin in place. She couldn't stop it; he continued to push, her lips came apart, the finger was inside her mouth.

'Bite,' he said. She felt it between the blades of her teeth. The tip of a finger is mostly bone; she could feel it just below his skin. Tears boiled in her eyes. In vain she tried to push away his hand. 'Bite it. You want to.' Which was true. Every nerve called for her to use her teeth, to clamp down as hard as possible. To bite through meat. What stopped her wasn't principle: she would have given him what he asked for. It was revulsion at the idea of flavor, the way a thing opens, flowers, once you begin to chew.

Claire doesn't know how long he held it there. He moved the finger from one corner of her mouth to the other, ticking across her teeth, even once tapping her tongue, which she immediately furled into the back of her mouth. Then, with a simple chuckle, he removed it. He didn't say anything about it afterward, and from that moment on Claire, who had tried once or twice to talk with him, to learn what he wanted, how she could bring the ordeal to an end, could no longer speak. He'd already called Paul, and while they continued to wait, before her neighbor happened to stop by, he sat across from her, pleased with himself, his jaw hanging in a wolfish grin.

As soon as he was gone, in the gap of time when she was at last alone, she furiously brushed her teeth, again and again and again, until she simply pumped the mint paste directly from the tube into her mouth and smeared it around with her tongue, trying to wash out the taste of his finger, the salt, sweat, tobacco, the sour taste of garbage, of decay.

Once more she feels on the edge of tears, before realizing, in a cold, compressed burst, that it isn't the consequences for Paul if she calls the police that should concern her: it is the consequences for herself if she doesn't.

So this is what's changed. As a divorced woman, the calculus of dependency between herself and others, between herself and Paul, has shifted. She wishes her ex-husband no harm. She hasn't ceased to love him, but that doesn't mean she owes him the kind of high, selfless loyalty he's asked for. When she slept with him — an event whose significance, if it ever had any, is now zero — it changed nothing about this new reality.

She doesn't know what they intend to do with it, but however Paul and his brother dispose of the body, someone will find it. They've embarked on this adventure as amateurs; there are details they will miss, they will leave behind a record of tonight's events and, however long it takes, the police will eventually reconstruct what happened, or a version of it, and then they will come knock on Claire's door: and then everything, everything she is, everything she wants to be, all the lustrous promise, everything will change. On the wall, immediately in her line of sight, hangs a gift from Bernard on the occasion of her hiring at the museum: a small pencil drawing by Schiele, of a gnarled, deathly hand, on cream-white paper. There are few possessions she prizes more.

Claire, ridiculously, is still dressed for a fancy evening. Wrinkles of fabric have gathered between her knees, where lines of light, like seams of ice, fill the creases. Smoothing them with her thumb, she recalls the circumstances which so recently surrounded her: the champagne, the conversation, the wealth and influence, the world to which she now belongs. It is a world of privilege, order, importance, responsibility. But it is one she earned. It belongs to her, also. She rises; it does not seem right to sit for this. Quieting the last alarms of guilt, Claire picks up her phone and presses the necessary buttons. She resigns herself to a future remorse, knowing that it is, it really is, the best of a terrible set of choices. In the end it is the best choice for everyone. She stands there, in the empty room, not yet certain of what she will say, waiting for a voice to come on the line.

Day breaks as they approach the city limits. Light begins to fill the car, a thick, heavily colored early-morning light. It is perverse that another day will begin as usual — that everyone in this city, most of whom haven't yet broken from sleep, will simply put on clothes, have breakfast, listen to the weather and traffic reports, converge in the ordinary way. The thought oppresses him. He shakes violently. It starts within, the plucking of individual nerves, like the testing, one by one, of a piano's wires, and then sprawls outward until at last it seems to be an external sensation, delirious and brutal. 'Do you want me to pull over? Should I stop the car?' The voice is his brother's. Ben, if anything, stands to lose more than Paul; underneath his words, in a low current, is a strain of desperation, a sticky throb of regret. The wish to unravel the knitted inevitability of present circumstance. How did a man, Ben must be wondering, with a kind of amazed anguish, how did a man, with as much stake in the wide, waking world as he has, consent to participate in such an undertaking? Paul shakes his head in response to the question. He looks past his brother and watches the rising sun. It is fully above the horizon now but hanging tentatively, as if fearful that at any moment the darkness might reappear and beat it back down into its coffin.

They drive on in silence, the brothers. The city is already visible, those first dark crops of housing projects, and they press forward, toward its heart. Soon they will be engulfed. The churn of the metropolis will absorb them completely. Later, when Paul is alone again, the hard weight will return. He has performed the act which most appalls him: he's taken a life. Even now it sits within him like a tumor, embedded, unremovable. Doctors and priests each practice their own methods of surgery but neither offers what Paul's situation calls for. He looks at Ben, who doesn't return the glance, and whose face has a restored rigidity. It is the same, strong collection of features Paul has always known.

He looks at himself in the car's side mirror and finds that the face there, his own, is also the same as yesterday's. But there is a change, both mental and deeply material; he senses it with a fine intuition of self. His skin is starched with a film of dry sweat. He'd like a shower, but what would be clean? His discomfort has no remedy; he belongs now to an entirely different class of people. He can't remember ever having been so fiercely aware of his own being – of the adjustment of a wrist, the small texture of skin, the pressure between two dry lips. He's never been more certain of the fact that he exists.

Ben drives faster, anxious to be done with this errand, and his eyes, under a beveled brow, indicate an absorption with his own thoughts. Even as he speculates about what those might be, Paul has trouble staying awake – everything in him is weary and sore, and for the first time in hours, though it seems like days and months, nothing is demanded of him; he drifts off. At a word from his brother, he comes to. Buoyant from the lightheadedness that follows a tatter of sleep, a sort of benign, startled curiosity, Paul asks what he has been thinking.

The city expands, filling the windshield, and Ben doesn't respond immediately; he simply watches. 'Nothing,' he says at last. 'Just something about Dad. Something that happened before you were born.'

Staring elsewhere, Paul goes to make a reply, then decides against it; he isn't quite sure what he would have said. Instead he sits next to his brother, not speaking, a silence crossing through silence, into the approaching city and its consuming grandeur. As it grows they shrink. The hour is still early, before the wild and uncertain heartbeat, the return to life, that morning brings: the closely huddled buildings of Manhattan have a severe, sacred dignity. They don't pretend to house God. But they too speak of the need – greater than vanity, graver than ambition – to be of use: the need not to be nothing. Sunlight, stronger now, burns behind them, and the city flames into brilliant silhouette. Everywhere, everywhere they rise, these structures of terrifying endurance, these towers that slice apart the sky. These cathedrals that everywhere men build.

ACKNOWLEDGMENTS

It's as simple as this — without their wisdom, intelligence, love, guidance, and unwavering belief, this book would not now exist: Samantha Holmes, Uzodinma Iweala, Jamaica Kincaid, and Chris Parris-Lamb.

I would also like to thank my editors, Stuart Williams and Alexis Washam, for their tremendous, patient work on my behalf, as well as my U.K. agent, Caspian Dennis.